I believed you.

A NOVEL BY

SHIRLEY GUENDLING

PRAISE FOR
I BELIEVED YOU

"Some time ago I had the privilege of reading
a preliminary draft of I Believed You. At that early stage,
I was thoroughly intrigued with the twisting, turning plot
and those charmingly quirky characters Cliff, Madeline
and Ernie. Well! Now after reading Shirley's completed,
published novel — it just got better and better! So proud
and excited to have been in on this from the ground floor."

– Ellie Hughes, Librarian Assistant

"A beautiful woman is murdered. The mortician doing
the autopsy realizes she is the woman he once loved. The
riveting 'whodunit' kept me on the edge of my seat from
the opening scene to the final page. You will love this
intriguing story too. Believe me."

– Heidi Roemer, Author of *Nine Books*

"Every time I turned a page, I was greeted with a new facet of this story. My thoughts traveled from one character to the next and the next, as I determined to unravel the answer of who was the psychopath. *I Believed You* will jerk you around and pull you deeply into the story as the writing toys with your suspicions. This is a fast, fun read that will take you into a clever, horrifying dimension."

– Hilary Jastram, Author of *Killing Karl*

"Wow oh wow! This was such a fun read. I felt the characters were real, and their needs and ultimate actions so unpredictable. Revenge always leads to disaster, and in this story that is exactly what happened. I loved it!"

– Jenny Taylor, Professional Photographer

For Marge

all the best

Hugs.

Shirley

I believed you.

A NOVEL BY

SHIRLEY
GUENDLING

Sterling
Forest
PRESS

I Believed You: A Novel

Copyright 2018 by Shirley Guendling

All rights reserved.

Published by Silver Tree Publishing, a division of
Silver Tree Communications, LLC (Kenosha, WI),
under its Sterling Forest Press literary imprint.

www.SilverTreeCommunications.com

Editing by:
Hilary Jastram
Kate Colbert

Cover design and typesetting by:
Courtney Hudson

First edition, July 2018

ISBN: 978-1-948238-04-5

Library of Congress Control Number: 2018949862

Created in the United States of America

DEDICATION

For Don, my late husband, for all his love and encouragement. And ... of course, for Hilary Jastram.

TABLE OF CONTENTS

Prologue
CLIFFORD

November 1984

I gripped the knife high above her slender body. My plastic apron made a crackling sound as I raised my arm.

The big glass door opened and my co-worker Annie entered. "If it isn't Clifford Wilson all suited up, and ready to start work," Annie chirped. "I was in here earlier to do my usual fantastic assist with this bodacious bod, but you were a no-show," Annie said. "So, are you ready now?" She cracked her gum vigorously.

I tore my gaze away from the nude body. "Sure," I mumbled weakly.

This autopsy room was no different from any other. It was cold and sterile with sleek steel tables, knives, and scalpels of all shapes and sizes. Of course, it had the usual saws, chisel, etc.

The room had the same odor of dead flesh it always had. No matter how hard we'd tried to remove it, that scent stuck. We'd used bleach, Lysol, and many other strong disinfectants.

When a visitor is in attendance, such as a reporter or relative of the deceased, we offer a cloth loaded with Noxema cream to help mask the sickening stench. "Hold it over your nose," Annie would instruct. "Maybe you will be able to escape the inevitable vomiting."

"You haven't even started the prelims yet? Why not? Late night? Or, you just hate to mess up the latest lovely?" Annie asked.

"Not a late night. Just the same feeling that comes over me before the first cut," I replied, trying to sound as nonchalant as possible, though my pulse raced in triple time. Sweat beaded on my forehead.

Maddie's body, even on my table, looked as beautiful as ever. Her long, silky hair draped over her shoulders and *oh, those gorgeous legs! This was going to be horrible!*

How had it ever come to this end?

Her perfect body had been photographed, X-rayed, re-photographed and measured. I could have told stories about every mark on Madeline's body. I had seen every inch of her many, many times ... hungrily.

My right eye twitched. *Damn. Such a sign of nerves and mine are raw.* I wanted to rip off my rubber gloves and run my hands over her smooth, creamy skin.

"Let's get to it," Annie said, cheerily, as she flipped the "on" button for the microphone hanging from the ceiling. Annie picked up her clipboard to take the notes I would dictate.

I hadn't realized how tightly I gripped the scalpel. The muscles in my hand cramped. I tried to relax a little. *Impossible,* my brain screamed.

The first cut was the "Y" incision to the chest. It took all my powers of concentration to keep my hand from shaking. Annie would have a lot of questions if she noticed.

Though I had done this procedure many times …

This time it was different.

THIS WAS MADELINE!!!

Chapter One
CLIFFORD

June 1984

When I met Maddie, I was just finishing up med school. I found out later; she was studying creative writing at the local community college. Both of our schools were in the Chicago area. She was 12 years younger than me, and I still had more school to complete.

I didn't know what she was studying to be. Was it an author of books, for a job in journalism? Or, maybe a job with a newspaper? Whatever, I thought it was great that we both had studying to do.

My acceptance to Loyola was the realization of a dream come true. It was everything I ever wanted, and all I cared about. Of course, those were my feelings *before* I'd met Madeline Manning.

I'd always had pretty good grades, in grade school and high school. Actually, I had been pushed ahead an entire year.

I wasn't aware then how that would help bridge the age gap between Maddie and me. Since she was so much younger than me, I sure didn't want to come off as an old "fud."

When I got to medical school, the grades didn't come easy. I would overload on the caffeine and stay up overnight, if necessary so that I could pass. I figured the headaches were a side effect of the caffeine, that it was all part of the package.

I didn't care. I had a goal in mind. I didn't intend to give up my dream of becoming a medical examiner.

As a kid, I'd wanted to be a doctor. I'd had many illnesses as a youngster, and I'd always wondered if the doctor had come up with the right diagnosis. I would ask my mom, on the way home, if she thought the doctor was correct. She thought that was a crazy question coming from a child, and also quite impertinent! "Of course, the doctor was correct," she would snap.

Boy, I missed a lot of school from measles, mumps, chicken pox, you name it … I had it!! My mom wanted to know why a kid would question a doctor. Most of the kids I knew felt a doctor's word was law. I guess the only answer I can think up is, after my doctors' visits, diagnoses, plus prescribed meds, I really didn't feel any better.

I've suffered from headaches for as long as I can remember. None of the prescriptions I've tried have helped. I wanted to be the kind of doctor who could get to the bottom of the problem and fix it!

I've always wondered if my headaches came because of a beating I'd gotten when I was seven years old, the time the front of my head was bashed on the playground. And this wasn't the usual concrete slab either, underfoot; our playground was made of a bunch of stones that hurt you like crazy if you tripped and fell.

One day, a couple of bullies ganged up on me and decided it would be fun to whack the local "goody two shoes" with a baseball bat. This was no lightweight baseball bat either. It was the heavy-duty kind. When I think back on that, I realize that whack could have killed me!

One guy was so fat I was surprised he had the strength to swing. The other guy was a short runt, and I was confused about why he would pick a fight unless he figured he could run like hell. The pain from the head injury was so bad I had thought it might kill me. *Maybe, it really was what caused the headaches?* Guess I'll never know for sure, but I don't remember having headaches before the hard smack on my forehead.

I wasn't the friendliest guy in school. I didn't want to associate with those bullies ... or anyone. It wasn't that I didn't like people, I've just always felt I was a little scant in the personality department. I would see other guys in a conversation, laughing, and having fun. And I was never sure I could "fit in."

The only teacher who came out that day, to see what was going on, was old Mr. Higgins. *What did he think he could do about it?* Mr. Higgins was so old and frail. He seemed frightened of everyone. *Poor guy.* Still, I had to give him credit for trying to break up those bullies. I'd always felt that he liked me. Maybe he understood about a guy being shy.

The thrashing hurt physically, but it also crushed my ego. I decided I would get back at those bullies by acting a little "crazy." I wanted those punks to fear me.

Whenever I saw them, I would walk goofy and flash a grin their way. I would even cross my eyes and try to drool!

I kept that act up until they were out of sight.

Also, I would tell them that I had read about some terrible car accident, that all the people had been killed! "Wasn't that hilarious?" They just looked at me oddly. I'm not sure if they feared me, but from then on, they were never sure how I would react to their teasing, so they stayed clear of me.

Moving ahead in school worked out okay; I was tall for my age and could keep up with my new classmates in my freshman year. I mean, academically, of course. Socially, not as much. I was always a little shy, as I've said, but that was the worst around girls.

In my sophomore biology class, I met a super cute girl and developed a big crush on her. But I wasn't sure how she felt about me.

Sometimes, I thought she flirted with me, but maybe it was that she was nice to everyone, and it didn't mean anything special. She seemed outgoing and friendly. I thought her long blonde hair was gorgeous, and that she had the sweetest smile I had ever seen!

One day, after class, I stopped Betty Lou out in the hall and asked her if she would like to go to the corner drugstore for a Coke. She smiled, and (*wowser!*) said yes! We each had one more class before school was over for the day, and I could hardly concentrate at my desk. I was so excited to have a "Coke date."

When class was over, we met outside the front door of the school and walked side by side to the drugstore. I didn't reach for her hand, though I sure wanted to.

The "date" went okay, and we mostly talked about school, and our class together. I asked Betty Lou if I could walk her home, and she said, "No, thank you. I have to go to the grocery for my mom on my way home."

That was it. We said goodbye, and I went on my way home. I was already planning on how I would ask her if she would like to go to the movies. Boy! I sure was moving ahead in my mind pretty fast. *We'd had only one Coke date, and I was planning a real date! Better slow down, Cliff!*

The weekend was coming up, so I would have a lot of time to decide, before our next class.

As usual, my mom had a lot of stuff for me to do around the house on the weekends. I would protest, claiming I had tons of homework, but she was very practiced at ignoring me.

When my mom had chores for me to do, she relished the idea of "lording it over me." No matter how much I protested, or how many excuses I came up with, her voice would get louder and louder, until she was just about at the shouting stage. When she got to that point, it always frightened me and made me furious at the same time. I would cover my ears and turn to leave the room, which angered Mom all the more, and she would shout "Clifford Wilson, don't you dare walk away from this room! How dare you turn your back on your mother?"

"Cliff, I need you to wash the outside windows. Before you know it, winter will be here, and then it will be too cold to wash windows. I need you to do it this weekend. No excuses or fake reasons. I certainly don't need any back talk either. Get busy. Now!!"

I really did have some homework, but it wasn't much. I could polish it off in a short time. So, it looked like I would be washing windows.

My mom was the boss in our house. She bossed my dad, and she bossed me. Dad was an easy-going guy. How and why he put up with Mom's demands, I'll never understand.

Although, Mom seemed to be a sweet young girl when she and my dad had met years ago (according to my dad).

He must've loved her when they met and married. From the stories they tell, it seemed that way, but it's hard for me to imagine her attractive and loving. Whatever my dad saw in her then has totally disappeared.

She was always so unhappy and ready to argue with anyone over ANYTHING. *Didn't she feel well?* When I was a lot younger, she paid attention to me, and everything I did seemed to make her happy. *What had happened? Why did she change? Had I changed?*

Dad worked hard as a mail carrier. He was friendly and knew most of the people on his route by their first name. As the years went by, and age took over, Dad's legs ached him constantly. He brought up that he wanted to leave his job to Mom often, and I could tell he was in pain by the way he limped around the house. Whenever he broached the subject, she would immediately harp that he could not retire yet. His pension would never be enough to cover all their expenses.

"What about Clifford's education? Have you forgotten his dream of being a doctor?" Mom asked, with a shrill tone.

"No, I haven't forgotten, but maybe I could find something else to do where I won't be on my feet all day, and my legs wouldn't hurt so bad?"

"What could you possibly do at your age? You don't have experience in anything else." Mom snapped back.

"I'm sure I could find something." Dad's voice shook when he responded to her.

I knew my dad wasn't feeling well, and he'd had a valid reason to bring up the subject of quitting the post office. He was almost pleading by that time, trying to convince my mom.

I hated to witness it, a grown man. My own father no less. Almost begging for a release from his obvious pain. He always rolled with the punches and never asked for much.

When he realized she wasn't budging, he dropped the subject.

One day, I decided to do a little jogging around the neighborhood. I was about two blocks away when I could not believe my eyes. Mrs. Wakefield, a widow lady, was holding her front door open and my dad walked IN!!! He stood there on her stoop, then and looked both ways. *That was a guilty move.*

Were they just friends? Were they having an affair?

My mind raced with all kinds of scenarios. Some good, some totally unbelievable!!!! If they were having an affair, I really couldn't blame my dad. I knew my mom made his life miserable. In some ways, I guess I would applaud him. But, wow!!! *This is blowing my mind!* I thought as I watched him with her. She was a nice-looking woman and had been a widow for many years. Finally, I decided that if they found something in each other, well, who was I to judge?

Mom was tall and not the most feminine woman in the world. She had lovely eyes, but a hard, square jaw, and heavy legs. Pictures of Mom tell the story of her younger struggles. Big bones, large feet, and coarse features did not make her an attractive girl.

Dad said she had never had a date in high school before meeting him in a department store. As Dad struggled over a large display of ties with a confused look on his face, he noticed a lady looking at the men's socks at the next display, and suddenly, blurted out: "Would you mind helping me choose a tie? I was invited to a party, and I have no idea what tie to choose. My suit is navy blue, and I am wearing a white shirt."

Mom told him she was pretty good with colors and would be happy to help. She smiled at him with the sweetest smile ever.

They decided on a navy and red stripe.

Next, my dad asked if she would like to accompany him to the party? She said "yes," almost a little too quickly, started chatting, and before either one realized it, they were laughing, talking, and smiling.

They enjoyed their time together at the party, and that was the beginning.

Dad came by the next Saturday and picked her up. She was not the mom I know now. They eloped three months later. Mom said she thought it would be more romantic to do it that way and Dad said they were broke. Mom chose Dad's tie for the wedding, too, and commented to him about how handsome he looked.

I knew Mom's childhood was not happy. Her dad left when she was seven years old. Every once in a while, she'd told me her mom would rave about what a bastard her father had been for abandoning her with a child. My grandma had been a dancer by the name of Miss Gladys with the Happy Bottom. Mom was completely embarrassed by her and didn't think her name was funny at all! Although, people in town thought it was hilarious.

My dad was the most ordinary looking guy you could ever imagine. Medium height, not overweight, not thin. His hair used to be light brown, according to the old photographs. Now it is thinning, and gray. He is still a good-looking guy, and I am sure many girls would have liked to go out with him when he was in his prime. That warm smile of his could've melted any girls heart.

So, it went that way in the house, off and on, Dad would bring up the same discussion, every so often, and nothing would be resolved. He was so unhappy with the way things were at home!

I did wash the windows, and I finished my homework that weekend. I even found time to call Pete, one of my buddies. We agreed to take in the local movie playing at our neighborhood theater. Pete wanted to see E.T. I would have preferred a horror or action movie. But I had chosen the movie last time, so I agreed.

I looked in my closet for my bell-bottom pants and found a jersey print shirt, which I thought looked okay for a movie. When I was finished dressing, I thought I didn't look too bad. Mom had been telling me I was a handsome boy since before I could remember. Now, I'd turned into a man with pretty good looks.

I must admit, I did enjoy the movie. The script was damn good, and the acting was pretty alright, too. Pete and I stopped for a burger on the way home. I knew it would spoil my appetite for dinner. But Mom would find something to nag at me about, no matter how much or little I ate. Pete was a funny guy, and he had me laughing at his comments about the movie. He wanted to know if I believed in aliens? *Did I?* I didn't know.

Finally, Monday rolled around, and all I could think about was getting to my biology class and seeing Betty Lou. I looked all over the classroom, and she wasn't there! I panicked! *Was she ill, did she quit the class?* I didn't even have her phone number!

At last, she rushed in, with apologies to Mr. Jenkins for being a couple of minutes late. Wow, what a relief for me.

After class, I went up to Betty Lou and asked how she was, how was her weekend, blah, blah, blah. Then I pulled myself up to my full six-foot height, swallowed and asked her if she would like to go to the movies the next Saturday.

I kid you not; she said, "Yes." I was plenty excited and said, "Do you have a particular movie you would like to see?"

"Oh yes," she said dreamily, I would love to see *"E. T."*

I couldn't believe it. Of all the pictures playing, she had to pick that one. I told her that sounded great, then got her phone number and address to pick her up.

I was going to have a real date with Betty Lou. Aliens be damned! I could sit through the movie again and pretend I had never seen it before!

I couldn't wait for Saturday. I shined my shoes and wore a fairly new shirt that no one at school had ever seen. When the day finally rolled around, and we had our date, it went well. I reached over and held her hand. I even had the feeling that Betty Lou really liked me. I certainly did like her!

We went to a local burger joint, and I was hoping someone from school would be there, to see how lucky I was, to have a date with Betty Lou! The only person in the restaurant was a gal who sat in the front row at school. She was a nosy kid and would spread gossip.

I knew the news of my date would be all over school.

I couldn't stop smiling.

Our Saturday routine started and went on for several weeks. We would catch a movie and then go for a burger. I was in heaven!

I had a little money of my own, from my work at the neighborhood drugstore where I stocked shelves and delivered prescriptions. It was the ideal job for me, considering my hopeful medical career. I learned the names of several drugs, what they were used for, and I memorized all the prescriptions by name.

I also worked occasionally at the local bookstore, which was another opportunity to learn medical terms. Whenever I was dusting shelves, and if we weren't too busy, I would open a medical book, and soak up any information I could.

I was proud to spend the money I had earned on Betty Lou. When we were together, I was careful not to push. The first couple weeks, I just held her hand. After that, I did slip my arm around her shoulders, during the movie. Then I finally ventured a small kiss, but that wasn't until our third date. She didn't resist, and I hoped she enjoyed the kiss as much as I did.

Then one day after class, Betty Lou said she was going to be busy the next Saturday. She didn't give any reason, and I didn't ask.

I was disappointed but figured it could be a family gathering that she'd been forced to attend. Little did I ever dream that she had a date with SOMEONE ELSE!!

The weekend finally ended, and I couldn't wait for school to resume! I wore my best shirt and pants again. I was hoping that would remind Betty Lou of the last time I'd worn them — on our first date.

I combed my hair three times. I wanted Betty Lou to think I looked pretty special.

After class, on Monday, I asked, "So, are we on for this next Saturday?"

Betty Lou held her books tightly against her chest. She wouldn't look me in the eyes and seemed frightened, as though I would sock her or something. I would never hit a girl, though when I heard what she said, the idea was appealing.

"No, Cliff, we won't be seeing each other anymore. I'm so sorry."

That was it. No explanation, nothing more than "so sorry."

I just couldn't get over the fact that Betty Lou had dumped me. Right out of the blue! No reason, no explanation.

It bugged me that no matter how many times I went over it in my mind, how our dates went, how we got along, AND how much she seemed to like me, I had no idea why she had given me the boot. *What the hell had gone wrong? Was she hooking up with another guy?* I needed some answers. Because I sure as hell didn't want a repeat of this kind of hurt ever again.

I was truly heartbroken. *I really cared about her and thought she felt the same. Nada!!!*

I started walking slowly past her house. During the day, I could see that nothing much was going on. I just assumed one or both of her parents were home. The family car was in the driveway, and the living room drapes were open. *But, what about Betty Lou? Was she at home? Was she making a date with that "new" guy?*

I did my "scoping things out" routine several times. It didn't really tell me anything. Why did I keep doing it? I don't know, but finally, I decided that if I wanted to find some answers, I would have to watch the house at night. Maybe even get inside! Now, I was thinking a little weird, and I knew it. But I didn't care.

I began walking by her house at night when it was super dark, and all the lights in the house were on.

One night, it was around seven o'clock, and I noticed that upstairs, her light was not on. The living room drapes were closed, and no car was in the driveway. *Did that mean they had all gone out? Would I dare break in?* I checked the front door, but not before looking around to see if any of the neighbors were out and about. No one was anywhere around.

The door was locked. I have to say; I was not surprised; Betty Lou's parents were very cautious people.

I tried several windows, and they were all locked. Finally, when I walked around to the back, I found a window over what I assumed was the laundry room.

I tried the laundry room window, and yep, it was unlocked! I opened it carefully and eased my way inside. The washer and dryer were right under the window, and I almost slipped to the floor when I landed on one of them. I looked around and listened for any sounds. None.

I walked carefully through the house, hoping there wasn't some loose animal, a dog or cat running around. I did figure though if a dog were in the house, it probably would've been barking its head off by then. No sound.

I made my way upstairs. I wanted to get in Betty Lou's room. Get inside her head.

I didn't have much trouble deciding which room was hers. Just like the curtains, everything was ruffly and pink. Like Betty Lou was, all ruffly and pink. *She was a perfect lady and a doll.*

I started looking around, hoping I would find a diary or something written about the guy. Nothing.

Then I noticed a flowery type calendar on her desk. I picked it up and went over the upcoming days.

Sure enough, there was an entry for next Saturday.

"Movies with Zach." So, that was his name. I didn't know any Zach at school. *Maybe he had already graduated? Maybe he was older and had a good paying job?* Hell, I was tired of guessing.

I decided I had better get out of there, while the gettin' was good.

Then I thought I heard a car pull up.

I went to the window at the back of the house, opened it, and jumped to the ground. I was lucky the ground was damp and soft. I could have broken my foot, or worse.

Wonder what they will think when they find an open window? Probably that someone in the family forgot to close it. Well, that was a scare. Not too bright of me, I might add.

What if I had been caught? I can't imagine what all would have happened. Would her mom and dad have called the police? Would I have been charged with trespassing? Probably, and that would have really messed things up for me. I would have to use better control.

I remember thinking: *I sure am doing a lot of screwy things lately.*

It was tough to see her in class each week, but slowly, and painfully, I learned to get over it, and HER!

Maybe stalking her for a little while helped to get her out of my system. I'd only done it because I wanted to see who the guy was that she liked better than me. I would hide across the street and wait for her to come outside with her date. He didn't appear to be so special. What did he have that I didn't? It would forever be a mystery.

I called her phone number and when she answered, I hung up. I wanted to scare her a little, or at least make her uncomfortable. I couldn't imagine what had happened to break us up. I hadn't gotten fresh (although I sure had wanted to). I had behaved like a perfect gentleman. *What the heck had gone wrong?*

I was reluctant about asking a girl out after that. I didn't want to experience that kind of hurt again.

But I did start dating again, and then was determined not to let my feelings run away with me. I was never what you would call a "ladies man," but I wasn't a dweeb either.

I am what people would describe as, a decent enough looking guy. I'm tall with light brown hair, hazel eyes, a soft voice, and impeccable manners. You would think I would have an easier time dating girls.

When my mom wasn't getting after me about a ridiculous, supposed shortcoming of mine, she would toss out, occasionally, and I do mean occasionally, a small compliment about my appearance. "You do have such nice eyes, Clifford, and I am so proud that you have my jaw."

I was always conscious of other people's feelings because I remembered how it felt when my feelings were hurt.

It seems I am always striving for acceptance, and maybe even love.

But I know my parents loved me. Especially my dad. He would broadly smile whenever I walked in the room, and always seemed happy to see me.

When I entered college, I felt I was, at last, on my way.

I was determined to make my parents proud. I realized the sacrifice they were making for me. They had scrimped and saved every dime.

Sure, the classes were tough, and the hours of study sometimes seemed to take over my life. I didn't care; I had my goal in mind. Social life could wait.

My college years were kind of blurry. I guess all work (and, as they say, "no play") didn't make for any real memorable moments. My life was books, study, and more books.

And I still suffered those damn headaches. That didn't help, and neither did the coffee or aspirin.

Fine, maybe too much beer here and there, in the past hadn't been the brightest idea. As I look back now, no wonder my memories are fuzzy.

Life and studying only intensified when I finally made it into medical school. It looked like, yes, I would become a doctor. And

I liked the sound of that in my head. I had dreamed about it long enough.

My headaches picked up in frequency and intensity. I had them nearly every day and blamed them on the hours I kept and the caffeine I downed. Sometimes, I popped something a little stronger than aspirin, too. I couldn't let the headaches slow me down! Nobody else knew, but I still had the prescription for the massive painkillers I'd had to take after I got whacked on the head. They kicked that pain down a good notch.

I kept telling myself once all the studying, long hours and scant sleep had stopped, the headaches would go away, and then everything would be fine.

Still, I knew my attitude and personality had changed.

I had always been a "good boy," and taught to do the right thing. I knew my mom and dad were proud of the way I conducted myself. I had always been considerate, even jovial!

Then I had changed. A lot of weird thoughts plagued my head that I couldn't seem to shake. I felt reckless at times, not caring what people thought of my actions. *What had happened to me? Why the total change?*

Researching "Trauma to the Frontal Lobe," brought me back to that hit I'd had years ago. I couldn't believe what I was reading!

Severe changes in personality may occur.

No longer caring what people think of one's actions.

Having thoughts of hurting people!

Never worrying what damage and hurt one's actions would cause.

I knew I was different and the reason for it existed in the book I had read. *Damn it anyway.* The whack on the front of my head that day on the playground had manifested into who I had become. I hardly recognized myself.

Mom picked up the change in me. No wonder she was always criticizing me. She used to be always praising me.

Holy shit!!

I dont care. That's who I am today. Too bad if people don't like it, or ME.

It was a good thing I had limited access to painkillers. I couldn't stand the lousy headaches without the scrips I'd prescribe for myself.

Good thing, too, I had moved out of Mom and Dad's house a while back. Having my own apartment gave me the freedom I craved, and the relief of not listening to the nagging, and negative comments from my mom. I did miss seeing Dad every day, and I know he missed me, too.

Contrary to all the horror stories about med school I'd heard, I did not find it terribly gross or gruesome. Lucky me, right?

The other students and I worked on cadavers, and while a few, found it totally repulsive, I did not. In fact, I found the dead bodies quite interesting. My fascination with the dead is what ultimately steered me to pathology.

Once or twice, I would sneak back into the lab where the corpses were. I would look them over and touch their cool skin, stare at their eyelids closed forever. As I lingered there, I would check them to see if I could find any wounds, bullet holes, or some reason for their death. If no clue could tell me how they'd died, I guessed they must've kicked off from some exotic disease. Sounds weird to say, I know, but I was intoxicated with the dead.

Then I met Madeline.

Chapter Two
CLIFFORD

June 1984

It was a nice spring day, and all the trees were budding. I was in a good mood and looking forward to seeing Ernie, and some other old friends.

I had ridden the bus to the far side of town. I wasn't usually in this area and wondered why Ernie had chosen this neighborhood. *Maybe the rent was cheaper? Or maybe it was closer to the gas station where he worked?*

When Ernie called to invite me to a "small get together" at his place, I couldn't believe it! We had not hung out in years, and after so much time had gone by, I wasn't sure if I would ever see him again.

I was feeling good about the idea of us hanging out when I entered the apartment. I saw several old friends and went around, shaking hands with the guys, and of course checking out all the gals.

That was the first time I saw Madeline, and I have to say, once I spotted her, everyone else just faded into the background.

She was the most gorgeous of all the girls I had ever seen, and I couldn't stop looking at her.

Briefly, I remembered that fiasco with Betty Lou and determined to keep a level head, and never fall so hard for any gal again.

Ernie's place was small and old. The window blinds yellowed and cracked.

Considering it was the mid-80s, I'd figured his apartment had been built sometime in the 1930s. It was quite deteriorated and way past its prime. Most of the furniture was hand-me-down décor and had cigarette burns on the cushions. The upholstery was so faded; hardly any colors were visible. A total dump.

I did notice a couple throw pillows on the couch that looked fairly new. And I had to admit; the place was clean.

Ernie had never been into housekeeping. When he first moved out of his parent's house, he'd had a one-room place. I was only there a couple of times, and it was always filthy. Dirty dishes in the sink and dirty clothes piled around the room.

Ernie never made the bed; that was just the way he was, but he was always happy to welcome visitors, and never gave a thought to what others felt about his place. As long as I'd known him, he has always been a happy-go-lucky kind of guy.

I don't remember any of the other party-goers that night except for Maddie and Ernie.

The room was dimly-lit, but candles burned everywhere.
I thought they smelled like ocean breezes.

A sound system played very softly, and I recognized "Truly" by
Lionel Richie. My eyes zeroed in on that gorgeous gal immediately. Her slender body moved gracefully around the room. Her
shimmering deep blue dress clung to her body in all the right
places. I couldn't tear my eyes away.

She walked up to me and greeted me with the sexiest voice
I'd ever heard! "Hi!" she said. A pink drink swirled in the glass
in her hand. Her fragrance was intoxicating. I stammered and
trying to dazzle her with my manliest, sexiest grin, croaked,
"Hi, right back at you." Sweat ran down my back, and I wished
I hadn't worn a sports jacket.

"Aren't you having anything to drink?" she asked.

I realized I didn't have a drink, and I needed one badly.

She had little left of her drink.

"How about I get you a fresh one? What are you
drinking?" I asked.

She smiled. "A Cosmo and this is my second, so I had better
pass." When her satin voice purred, I was a goner.

I returned with my drink (a Cosmo, of course, even though I hate
that kind of drink — I wanted that gorgeous woman to think we
had something in common).

On my wobbly walk back in her direction, I noticed her legs again. *Her gorgeous legs.* Christ, did I need that drink! Cosmo or not, I was feeling shaky and nervous as a schoolboy about to lose his virginity. "Hang on buddy, keep your head on straight. Play it cool." I whispered under my breath.

"So, what's your name?" I asked.

She answered in her musical voice, "My name is Madeline, but my friends call me Maddie."

"Well, then," I stammered, "May I be presumptuous and also call you Maddie?"

She smiled a coy (*did I say coy? What is this woman doing to me?*) smile, and said, "Of course."

I extended my free hand even though it was sweaty, and said, "I'm Cliff." Suddenly, I hated my name. I wished I could have said, "Hi, I'm Brock," or "I'm Clay." Or, some other rugged male-sounding name.

She replied, "Hi, Cliff." *Amazing!! Wow!!!*

We finished our drinks, and when I offered to get a refill again, she said, "I guess, one more won't hurt." We sipped our drinks slowly, and I thought she was the most breathtaking creature I had ever seen!

We continued our small talk which came easily. "What do you do? Where do you work? Blah, blah, blah."

I refreshed our Cosmos. God, I couldn't believe I was having a second. *I'm dying for an Old Style*, I thought.

The music played softly, and I became more interested by the minute!

We talked a little more, and I asked if she would like to dance. She told me, "No, not this time."

Does that mean there will be another time? I swallowed the lump in my throat as big as Gibraltar. Then I said, "May I have your telephone number, so we can set up the next time?"

"I'll be happy to see you again, Cliff," she said. "Though I prefer to call you. I enjoyed meeting you, and our 'getting to know you' talk."

When Madeline said my name, it suddenly *did* sound sexy and masculine.

That was a different angle, her calling me, but I figured, what the heck? If I got to see her again, that was all that really mattered.

I wrote my name and number on a soggy cocktail napkin and handed it to her. Her eyes swept over the napkin. She looked up and purred again, "I'll call you."

Would she really call me?

Then she excused herself. I thought she was only going to the ladies' room, but I didn't see her for the rest of the night.

She just vanished!

I found Ernie deeply engrossed in a blonde hottie and interrupted him with an apology. "I'm sorry to barge in Ern, but who is this Madeline, and how do you know her?"

"I don't know her. Sandy brought her," Ernie said. "I've never seen her before tonight. Pretty damn good looking huh? How did the two of you get along? Did you get her number?"

"I asked, of course, but she wouldn't give it to me. Said she would call me. How's that for a switcheroo? Wonder if I will ever hear from her again? I thought she was plenty hot!!!"

He smiled.

"Where's Sandy?" I asked.

"She left about 20 minutes ago."

Ernie sounded annoyed. Couldn't blame him for that. I had paused his progress with the blonde.

I had just met the girl of my dreams, and I didn't know how to contact her OR if she would ever call me.

I checked my watch, and thought, *kinda early for her to end the evening. Was she seeing someone later? Why should it bother me?*

It did.

I dumped the rest of the Cosmo and left the party, desperately in need of an Old Style.

Chapter Three

MADELINE

July 1974

I grew up in a small town as an only child. My mom and dad divorced, and I knew so little about boys or men.

I was curious about boys, although I had no idea what they were thinking or what might be interesting to them. Probably sports was number one on their list?

That was wrong; I soon figured out. After reading a lot of movie magazines, I soon realized SEX was the number one thing on all boys' minds.

"Sex," I wondered aloud. "What is that all about?"

I wasn't in a big hurry to find out.

My mother doted on me. She tried to give me everything she had been denied as a child. Any extra money she had, she would use to buy the prettiest clothes she could afford.

I was a cute little girl. And Mom wasn't the only one that thought so.

When we would go into a store, we would hear people exclaim, "What a pretty girl you are! Look at those beautiful curls, and dimples, too! My, my, a real little beauty!"

Hearing that made me self-conscious, but I loved the attention all the same!

I didn't have a brilliant mind, but I passed each grade. I never had top grades, but I always managed to move up to the next grade. Thankfully. I wanted Mom always to be proud of me, and not just because I was a "pretty little girl!"

"Being attractive may open some doors, but not all." I soon figured that phrase to be true. I had to work extra hard on my school work, to keep up. I supposed the other kids didn't have that much of a struggle.

Writing was a relief. I wrote poems and short stories when I was in school. My teachers praised my writing and my efforts.

I just knew that one day, I would become a famous author! *How great would that be?* Mom would really be proud of me then.

When I finished high school, I took a boring job in an insurance agency, and learned numbers definitely were NOT my thing.

I was taking creative writing classes in the evening at the local community college. My hopes still clinging to becoming a writer.

Then I found a job at a local greeting card shop. I worked there on the weekends and didn't make much money, but I liked the job.

I would read the greetings in the cards, and get ideas for poems, and short stories. That was so much fun!

I knew I couldn't exactly "copy" the sentiments in the cards, but I sure could get inspiration! Who knows? Maybe I'd end up working for Hallmark someday!

Doesn't hurt to dream, I told myself. *I might as well dream BIG!!!*

Chapter Four
CLIFFORD

June 1984

The next day and night, I was foolish enough to think Madeline would call me right away. She didn't. *Why would I even think that?* She probably had a dozen guys waiting to take her out! I certainly can't be the most appealing guy she'd ever met. *Well, the hell with her. I don't care if she calls or not.* "Who am I kidding?" I sighed. I did care.

As the days rolled by, I lost all hope of ever seeing her beauty again.

The anxious waiting began. I sat at my desk trying to study. I had a huge paper to write and was getting nowhere. *What the hell has happened to me?* I didn't even know her. I had *never* acted this way before. Problem was, every time I thought of her, I knew I was behaving like a boy of 13 with a recurring erection. *Ridiculous!*

I called Ernie several times, asking if he had heard anything more about the mysterious Madeline, or if he had talked to Sandy. His answer was always the same: "Negative."

I didn't know if I should be disgusted or angry.

What kind of a stupid game was she playing?

The headaches returned. I downed aspirin continuously, then slumped into a depression. I was feeling so bad; I didn't care if I showered or shaved. And I knew I was acting like a jerk. There were plenty of other beautiful girls on the planet. *Why was this one so special?*

Sure, I still hit the books, but I didn't absorb much. I read and re-read the same pages over and over.

A week went by. Finally, on Monday, the phone rang. I swear it had a different ring. My voice sounded juvenile in the empty room as I answered it.

"Hello, Cliff. This is Maddie. We met at Ernie's party. Do you remember me? How are you?"

Did she really think she had to explain where we had met? *Was she crazy? Did I remember? Oh man, did I remember!*

"Yes, I remember you, Maddie." I hoped I sounded casual. "It was at Ernie's place, right?" My eye twitched, and I scolded myself for asking her about what she had just told me. *Get a grip!* Talk about a case of nerves. Good thing she couldn't see me. "I'm glad you called," I managed.

"Really? Are you?" she asked teasingly.

"Yes, in fact, I was hoping you would call before the weekend. I have concert tickets for next Sunday night, and I wanted to ask you to go with me."

"How nice," Maddie said. "What concert?"

"The Moody Blues at Poplar Creek. Do you like The Moody Blues?"

"I adore them," sighed Maddie. "I would love to go with you. I will definitely be looking forward to this! I saw in the paper that they would be appearing close by in town. How very nice of you to invite me. Thank you, Cliff."

My spirits soared! I'd scored with the beauty, and maybe she liked me, too! (*Or was it that she really did like The Moody Blues, and would have been happy to go see them with almost anyone?*)

I couldn't think that way. All I wanted to dwell on was that I'd asked Madeline for a date, and she'd accepted!

"How about dinner first? I know a great Italian place with the best red wine. I mean, Cosmos." I laughed to cover my error. "They also have the best pasta around."

"That sounds perfect, Cliff." When she said my name again, it was a turn on. *Crazy.*

"Tell me the time and the place, and I'll be there."

"I would be more than happy to pick you up," I said. "Just give me your address."

"No, Cliff," Maddie replied a bit rigidly. "If you don't mind, I prefer to meet you. After all, we hardly know each other."

What else could I do? I told her the name of the restaurant and where it was located, and we settled on the time.

The days dragged until the day of our date. I wore my dressiest shirt and pants and shaved as close as I dared. I did splash aftershave on, not too much, I hoped. When I walked into the restaurant, Maddie was standing at the hostess station.

Damn! I'd wanted to get there first to make a good impression that I was a perfect gentleman. I wanted it to look like I would be in charge of the evening. (Even though, I knew I would follow her lead.)

She wore a red sweater and pants. I was disappointed she wasn't in a short skirt or dress to show off those legs. But heck, the sweater was tight, and she was her usual gorgeous self. Seeing her set my mood off in high spirits. I had big plans for the two of us, even though I knew I was planning way too far into the future. *So, what?* I couldn't help it. Those thoughts made me feel great!

The hostess took us to a quiet, small table in the rear of the restaurant.

This is going to be one fabulous evening.

I was happy she'd agreed to the red wine and hoped it would have the same effect on her that it always had on me.

We each ordered the "special." I didn't care how much I spent on the dinner; this was going to be one spectacular evening.

We soon realized that we had so much in common.

"Do you like beets? Do you eat most vegetables?"

"Do you have a sweet tooth?"

"Which movie would you vote as your most favorite?"

I was so happy that almost all the answers she gave were the same as mine.

We ate slowly, and the conversation flowed so easily.

I was really enjoying myself. I couldn't believe she had finally called me, and we were on our first date.

I sure as hell hoped it wouldn't be our last!

I didn't want the dinner to end because we just seemed to "click."

If I made an attempt at telling a small corny joke, she laughed as though she'd genuinely enjoyed it.

It was hard to concentrate on my pasta. I wanted to keep looking at her beautiful face.

I offered more wine and suspected she was becoming as relaxed as I was.

We made it to the show on time, and I wished we hadn't broken the mood of what we'd had going at the restaurant.

I had bought the best seats I could afford.

She loved the show. I could tell. It felt like I had scored a home run! (Even though I wasn't sure.) She was easy to be with, but still, a little, reserved.

I couldn't put my finger on what it was. She was different than any other gal I had dated. And … the most beautiful!

After the show, I suggested we go for a nightcap.

Maddie agreed, and my hopes for what might happen later in the evening soared!

We found a small bar near the theater and had another glass of wine. My hopes went higher!

After we finished our drinks, I asked Maddie if she would like some more wine.

"Thank you, but no, Cliff. I should be getting home."

"May I, at least, drive you?" I said, knowing I sounded too anxious.

"Cliff, that's so sweet. But as I said, we hardly know each other. Maybe some other time."

I tried not to show my disappointment, though my stomach and heart sank.

I stood and offered to help with her jacket. She leaned in and gave me a quick peck on the cheek. "Thanks for a lovely evening. I had a great time."

"Me, too. May I call you?"

"I will call you," she said twirling her hair. "Thanks again."

I wonder what would happen if I followed her?

She would probably be furious with me, and never see me again.

With that, she turned and walked out of the bar. *Damn, maybe it was something I said or did? Maybe she was being mysterious?* Whatever it was, I was back to my agonizing routine of waiting next to the phone.

Almost another week went by without a call from Maddie.

I was losing patience, but at the same time, not willing to give up. *NO! NEVER!!*

What in the hell is the matter with me? I was a wreck. I knew the answer, of course. I was falling or had fallen in LOVE!!! I hardly knew the gal, and I thought it was the real thing? *Could it really be love when we had met such a short time ago?*

Our next date took place at another restaurant close to my apartment. She was there, waiting for me, like last time.

And just like last time, she was beautiful. But this time, Maddie wore a short skirt. *Ah, those gorgeous legs.* I tried not to stare.

Again, we were seated in a quiet corner, and the wine and conversation flowed easily.

After dinner and a lot of wine, I asked if she would like to come back to my place. Then I almost passed out when she said, "Yes, that sounds nice. Do you live far from here?"

I told her, "Maybe a 20-minute drive."

I have Maddie sitting next to me, in my car. I tried to keep my mind on my driving, but it wasn't easy. My mind was full of so many wonderful, and exciting thoughts!

In anticipation that she might agree, I had all the tunes ready and had some scented candles of my own, not ocean breezes but not bad.

I had always kept the place neat and clean, but I'd really given everything an extra scrubbing. I vacuumed and made sure the bathroom looked good, too, in case she would need to go in there. Before I left to go to the restaurant, I double checked everything.

The new comforter and fluffy rugs made it nearly perfect. I had double checked the fridge and the wine cabinet.

When we got back to my place, I lit the candles and turned out all the other lights. Maybe I was a little transparent, but

I couldn't help it. I wanted everything to go without a hitch. I wanted Madeline to have feelings for me. Maybe it was too soon to hope her feelings would match mine, but at least, she could develop some good feelings about *us*!

I had opened a new bottle of medium priced red, hoping she would like it. I wanted Maddie to feel relaxed.

Maddie sat down on the sofa, and I inched next to her as close as I dared. She wore the same fragrance that drove me wild!

We sipped more wine. Finally, I gathered my courage, reached over and took her hand. "I think you are beyond wonderful," I said. *Did that sound corny?* It seemed so much of what I said sounded that way. I was always searching for just the right words.

To my ears, my voice sounded high pitched, when I really wanted to come off with a deep sexy tone.

Her eyes lit up. I grabbed the moment and kissed her. Soft and slowly at first, then passionately.

Maddie didn't resist, and the kisses kept coming.

I remember putting my arms around her and holding her as close as I could.

I don't actually remember leading Maddie to the bedroom, though, but I guess I did because the next thing I knew …

We undressed each other slowly, never losing eye contact. All the juices were flowing. I knew I had to take it slow. That wouldn't be easy, but, it was mandatory!

I wanted Maddie to enjoy our sex together. There was never any question about my enjoyment! Things were heating up for both of us! I could feel her responding, and that just added to my excitement.

I felt like I was climbing higher and higher. I tried to slow down, but suddenly I left earth and rocketed into outer space. I circled there, for, I don't know how long, never wanting to return. When people say, "I was in heaven," I think maybe that is where I was.

Slowly, our breathing returned to normal. We looked at each other, with complete satisfaction on our faces.

Sex had NEVER been that sensational before! NEVER!!!

So, it began. The most fast-paced, strenuous, physical love affair. I couldn't get enough of Maddie. Each time, our love-making intensified. It was crazy, intoxicating, exhausting and unbelievable.

Was I truly falling in love? Did she feel the same way?

It was hard to figure out Madeline.

She was always a little mysterious. I was never invited to Maddie's apartment. After an eternity of waiting, she had finally given me a phone number, but each time I called, there was no answer.

When she would call me, we would arrange to meet. I didn't like the mystery (or did it add to the excitement?), but I went along with it anyway because she wanted it that way.

Madeline was beautiful. Not movie star beautiful, but beautiful in an exotic way. Her long, dark hair smelled like a fragrance from a faraway place, incense-like. Her gray eyes were kind and a little sad. You could never be certain what she was thinking. Her eyes gave away nothing. Her mouth was full, and she always wore that shiny stuff on her lips. I couldn't wait to kiss it off!

One day, I questioned her about Sandy. "Are you and Sandy good friends?"

Madeline smiled and said, "Unfortunately, Sandy moved to California. We weren't close, but maybe I'll visit her someday."

Of course, I hoped that would never happen. How could I live without seeing Maddie, even for a few days? I figured a trip out west would involve more days than a few.

Our dates became more regular, and I certainly didn't want that to change.

My grades slipped. I was in the homestretch, and I couldn't let that happen because I had studied all those years. I did not take that lightly and was worried, but what could I do? Whenever Maddie called, no matter how hard I was supposed to be hitting the books, I dropped everything and hurried to see her! I told myself over and over; *there's no time to quit now, Cliff. You're almost to the finish line.*

The more Maddie and I dated the more I wondered if I could convince her to move to my place. That would be the ultimate for me. Maddie living with me! Total paradise!

One Saturday morning, I visited Mom and Dad. I had been seeing them less and less. I knew they missed me.

"How are your classes going?" Mom always asked.

"Just great," I lied.

They would be disappointed knowing my number one priority was Madeline. It would be a big concern for them if they thought I was letting my studies, and grades slip. They had expressed so many times how very proud they were of me. I didn't think they would be so proud of me anymore.

"Have you met any new, nice young ladies, Clifford?" (My mother's constant question.) I fibbed again. "Not yet, Mom."

Dad and I often had conversations about sports, but I'm sure he was picking up on the fact I wasn't nearly as well-versed on the subject as I had been in the past. Dad had his favorites, and he voiced his opinion when his teams weren't playing up to snuff. His stock comment was laced with disappointment, "What can you do? I'll still watch them, win or lose."

What would they think of Madeline? She would seem aloof. I had to admit she did come off as being older, even though she wasn't.

My folks would like it that I was dating a younger woman, but not someone who was aloof, or seemingly mysterious. You always knew where you stood with my straightforward parents.

I couldn't worry about if they would like her, not when I was more concerned with figuring out how to keep seeing Madeline! Also, like it or not, I had to get my grades back up. Even though Maddie was my first priority, I still wanted to be a medical examiner. How I was going to accomplish both was beyond me. I had to get that degree, and I couldn't lose Madeline. But my feelings for her were growing deeper.

Somehow, I managed to make it to graduation, and I even got the job as the pathologist's assistant I had interviewed for a few weeks before. I would be working closely with the most prestigious, sought-after, hospital. *My dreams were coming true!*

Maddie and I were becoming a regular couple. I was drawn to her. It wasn't just the sex. As amazing as that was, we had a real connection. We liked the same shows, the same foods. (One exception … I still didn't like having a Cosmopolitan drink.) We usually drank wine together, and that was fine with me.

I wasn't seeing much of Ernie either. We had been friends on and off for years. Mostly on, but once a couple years back, it was definitely off! Since we'd started talking again, it was the same but different.

Ernie seemed a little, what should I call it, guarded??

Our conversations followed the pattern that Ernie was always careful now of what he had to say. That certainly wasn't the way it was before. He seemed to be measuring his sentences, and words, but we'd never worried in the past about what we'd said to each other. We'd always just told it like it was.

Ernie had changed over the years; I suppose I had, too.

I was so happy that we were friends again. I still felt lousy about what I had done to him years ago.

Here's what happened.

Chapter Five
CLIFFORD

April 1984

Years ago, (when Ernie and I were close buddies), Ernie had met a new gal, and he had flipped over her.

"I just can't get to first base," he would moan. "I try to be everything a gal would want. You know, attentive, charming, humorous, whatever, and nothing clicks."

"Geez, Ern, are you sure she is worth you feeling ... so bummed?" Ernie went on to explain, how deep his feelings were for Yvonne.

"Wish I could do something to help you out. I have an idea, though. Want to hear it?"

Ernie nodded.

"Why don't you let me ask her out, and I'll put in a good word for you?" I suggested. "I can talk you up, about what a great guy you are. You know, all the bullshit girls like. I could go on and on about how caring you are, how much fun you are to be with, and I could throw in ... not too bad looking either."

"Do you think that would work?" Ernie asked. "I mean, I'll take it. I am really nuts about Yvonne. I sure do need help with convincing her to have 'real' feelings for me."

"Okay, now I get it," I said. "You *are* nuts about her."

"Obviously!"

"So, that's why you've been acting all weird," I teased. "She was at one of the beer parties, right?"

"Yes," Ernie said, looking as dreamy as Ernie could look. It was a bizarre expression for him. "Dude, I think I'm in love. I just need her to fall for me. Are you sure you can convince her? I want her to think I am the best catch in town!"

"I will pipe you up like you're Robert Redford or somebody hot like that." I said that last part under my breath.

Ernie gave me Yvonne's phone number and told me to keep him up to date on how it was going. "I will be sweating this out." He said with an odd expression. *Could ol' Ernie really be in love?* His reputation was that he liked to play the field. A different girl each week.

I called Yvonne when I got home and arranged to pick her up at her apartment the following evening. I had nothing but the best intentions, anxious to help out my pal.

We went to a local restaurant, and I ordered an inexpensive priced red. As we polished it off, her features softened.

Not that she was bad looking, to begin with, but with the candlelight, (and the wine) she looked so pretty. She did have a spectacular figure, but I wasn't sure how the conversation would go, and what we could possibly talk about. (Other than Ernie, of course!)

"So, Cliff, what prompted you to call me?" she said, almost whispering, in a throaty, sexy voice. I almost choked on my breadstick. *Where had that voice come from?*

"First of all, you are one heck of an attractive gal, and I just wanted to get to know you." I had planned on starting with that line and then inserting all the swell stuff about Ernie after she felt like we were friends.

But then ... I couldn't believe it! She just got better and better looking, and boy was she coming on to me!

"Cliff, I hoped for the longest time that you would ask me out," she gushed. "I've liked you for ages. I always thought you were one the best-looking guys in town. I liked the idea that you were educated and studying to be a doctor no less! I still can't believe you asked *me* for a date!"

I have to admit; it wasn't tough listening to her give me a ton of compliments. (*No worries about conversation now!*) What a great ego trip for me!

But, Jesus, now what? I knew I should nip it in the bud. Still, I couldn't help but wonder how far it could go. After a slow and lazy dinner of pasta topped off with more wine, we went back to her place.

She had a nice apartment. Clean and comfortable. *Score more points for Yvonne!*

Then she led me to the bedroom where she put on some romantic music. She had my shirt and pants off before I knew what hit me.

We had fantastic sex, and I hated myself and enjoyed myself at the same time. She was beyond skilled in bed, and I sure could see why Ernie was so gone over her. She had more experience than most girls her age.

We started spending a lot of time together, mostly in bed. I knew I was being a shit. *I will get to pumping up Ernie later.* At least, that's what I told myself.

Naturally, Ernie wanted to know how it had gone, and I told him, "Ern. I'm working on her, but it may take a little time. I don't want her to know it's a setup. Hang on. It will happen."

Finally, my conscience got the best of me. Poor Ernie was miserable, and I was, too, sort of. I knew I had to end it and get on with the real reason I was seeing Yvonne.

I started talking about Ernie. What a great guy he was, and that we are such good friends. "You would have to search plenty of places to find a better guy than Ernie," I emphasized.

I suggested that she and Ern give it a try.

None of that registered with Yvonne.

When I attempted to slow things down, she would have none of it. Talk about having a "hissy fit," I thought she was about to stamp her feet, and maybe start bawling!

"I have fallen in love with you, Cliff. Don't make noises about taking things slowly. I can't live without you, and I know you love me, too." I didn't say any more on the subject that night, merely kissed her lightly on the cheek, and left.

I stopped calling her and what do you think she did? Spilled the beans about us to Ernie. She had quite the story for him and then she called it quits with Ernie, too! For a while, I thought he might kill me. Guess I couldn't blame him for those feelings. I was supposed to help him out with Yvonne, make sure she wanted to be his best gal. Now, I had soured the entire relationship.

I know Ernie wanted to punch my lights out. Who could blame him? All three of us were miserable. I felt pretty lousy about all of it. Of course, I never saw Yvonne again, and …

I didn't see Ernie for a long time either.

Now, I can look back on those times and finally realize what pain I had inflicted on Ern. He had truly been in love, and I had screwed it up royally.

I still can't believe he finally came back around to acknowledge my presence. We were buddies once again. It wasn't the same as before, but at least he was speaking to me. *How long had it been since we'd had that big drama fest?* Five years? Of course, everything was forgiven. *Or was it?* I always wondered about that.

Chapter Six
CLIFFORD

June 1984

No one knew about Madeline and me, and she wanted it that way. I didn't really mind because I could have her all to myself then. I would have killed to show her off. People would have been amazed that "straight arrow" Cliff had such a fantasy girlfriend. Maddie was exotic; I was ordinary. She was sexy, in a vulnerable way. I was okay looking in a regular-kinda-guy way. That was my take on it anyway.

Was she my girlfriend? Was she seeing someone else? Why all the mystery?

That part of our relationship frustrated me.

One evening, in my apartment, after polishing off two microwave dinners, washed down with a couple of beers, I said, "Maddie, I would love to tell the whole world about us. Why can't I ever pick you up at your apartment? Why don't you ever invite me over?"

"Cliff," she said, looking directly into my eyes, "There are so many reasons, but none of them affect the way I feel about you." I nodded my head slightly as she continued, "First of all, I am a very private person. Second, my roommate doesn't like company, and the place is usually a mess. I would be embarrassed to have you see it." I stared at the floor instead of her alluring eyes and she rushed on, "Give me a little more time. Things will change."

I challenged her gaze when I answered, "Things will change how?" I worried she meant change as in "adios."

She just shook her head and said "Let's not discuss this anymore tonight. Things will all be resolved."

Then I decided not to pursue the subject further. Although, I hated that word "change." *What did Maddie mean?*

I was irritated, but not enough to stop seeing her.

My frustration always led me back to the way I had betrayed Ernie. Love was not easy, and I was in the middle of torture due to my situation. *What had he felt like? Had it been worse?* I had caused him so much agony. In those moments, it was hard to like myself.

Ernie was a middle-of-the-road kind of guy. Not bad looking, but no heartthrob either. He had a medium build, sandy-colored hair and light brown eyes. He was perfectly happy settling for average but too quick to laugh at corny jokes. He was just a nice, well-rounded guy. Since I had stomped on his heart with the whole Yvonne fiasco, he hadn't dated anyone … not seriously anyway, and I didn't count that blonde at his party. *Maybe he had sworn off women altogether? Could I blame him?* Everything I had lied to him about had happened years ago, but it had rocked Ernie hard. Who knew what kind of shape I had left him in?

Chapter Seven

MADELINE

May 1984

The greeting card company had a picnic one day that summer, and a local baseball team played.

I thought it would be fun to go, so I went by myself.

Boys came up to me and asked for my phone number, but none of them really appealed to me at the time.

I was still hurting over losing Gordon three years back. Gordon had been the sweetest guy in the entire world. We'd dated for about five months when Gordon asked me to marry him! I was beyond thrilled and accepted! I remained a virgin, and Gordon respected my decision. He knew I was saving "it" for our wedding night.

About one month before the wedding, Gordon was in a terrible car crash, and he did not survive.

To say that my world crumbled is an understatement.

I was heartbroken and devastated on a level I had never experienced. I knew I could never love another guy the way I had loved Gordon.

Truthfully, I wasn't interested in meeting new guys. But as the years rolled by, I realized I couldn't go on grieving for the rest of my life!

Believe it or not, even my mother had approved of Gordon.

When the game was over, a man came by. He was on the baseball team and sauntered in my direction with the sweetest grin. We talked awhile, and he told me his name was Ernie. "You're a gorgeous girl," he said. "I would love to take you on a date." He seemed so genuine even though I could tell he was rough around the edges, the proverbial "bad boy." He was totally different than Gordon, and I felt maybe that would be the best, no more comparing everyone to Gordon.

Maybe he's the type I've been looking for all along?

We started dating, exclusively, I might add. I wasn't seeing anyone else, and Ernie wasn't either. We had so much fun together. A lot of laughs, and plain old good times.

One night, we took in a movie with burgers and beers.

Another night, a nice restaurant, with a delicious dinner.

We even went roller skating. I wasn't very good, but Ernie kept his arm around me so that I wouldn't fall.

He was so sweet, and always taking care of me.

I certainly was one happy girl.

I thought maybe I was falling in love.

How could that be? I didn't think I could ever love anyone again!

I knew that I liked Ernie, and I enjoyed being with him. I felt secure, and so loved! *But, was this love?*

One night, he picked me up after work. We had hamburgers, and Ernie had more beer than usual. He was extra loving, and I guessed the reason.

When we finished with our burgers and beer, Ernie suggested we go back to his place. I knew he had sex on his mind.

When Ernie opened the door to his apartment, I was shocked. And not in a good way.

The place was dark, the furniture a disaster. But, I told myself, *maybe this is how all guys live?*

Ernie went to the fridge and opened two beers. Then he put his arms around me and gave me a long, passionate kiss. When he crushed me hard to his body, I could feel his erection.

"Come with me, my beautiful doll. Let Ern make you feel real good!" Ernie said in a low, and husky voice. Then he slowly steered me in the direction of the bedroom.

I wasn't sure I wanted to have sex, and I wasn't sure I didn't. I still had it in my head that I would wait until my wedding night. (Maybe I was being old-fashioned and foolish!)

We undressed slowly, and he kept staring at me with longing or hunger. I'm not sure which.

But every time he kissed me or talked close to my face the smell of the onions he'd had with his burger intensified.

That wasn't very considerate of him. He was planning on having sex and knew I was a virgin. You would think he would make it caring and romantic — without onions!!!

Ernie didn't have any candles, and he didn't play any romantic music. He had no idea how to create a romantic setting. Maybe that's the way with all guys?

Not that I was a decorating expert or anything like that, but it seemed to me, all Ernie had on his mind was satisfying his sexual urges. Was he even considering my feelings? Did he really love me, or was I just some gal that he'd hooked up with, to eventually coax into his bed? So many questions swirled in my head.

I tried to overlook the lack of attention he had put into everything. After all, this was Ernie, and thoughtful actions were not his strong suit.

I loved him. *Or did I?*

We climbed on the bed, and he murmured words
I couldn't quite make out.

I told myself he was saying he loved me.

"Ernie, take it slow. Remember, I'm a virgin," I said.

"Oh babe, I know, and ol' Ern's going to be as gentle as a feather
blowing in the breeze. How does that sound?"

"Ernie, I do love you, but I am a little nervous about this."

"I love you, too, sweets. Don't ever forget that."

Next thing I knew he was on top of me.

"You are heavy," I protested.

"Love, I'll be off in a minute."

He wasn't kidding. He thrust himself inside me, made a growling
sound, and then rolled off.

"It" was all over in a matter of seconds. *Is that how sex is
supposed to be?*

I was confused and very disappointed.

"Let's get dressed and have another beer," he said with a big grin.
"Then, I'll take you home. I don't mind telling you; you are more
beautiful than I could have ever imagined."

Ernie said he would make me feel good.

Instead, I felt terrible! I was so sorry I had ever let it happen.

I got up from the bed, trying to avoid thinking about how long ago the sheets had been washed — probably weeks ago, or maybe longer. They were so smelly and dirty. Gross!

I went into the bathroom, to clean up, and started crying. Silently, of course, so that Ernie wouldn't hear me.

"That was disgusting," I whispered to the mirror.

Ernie was still in the bedroom, finishing getting dressed, and hollered, "Come on hon! I'm waiting on you. Let's have that beer."

I didn't want a beer. All I wanted was to get out of there, so I could try and forget the whole fiasco had ever happened. To think I had given up my virginity, after all the beautiful ways I had imagined how it would be.

I finally finished dressing, walked into the kitchen, and I saw Ernie with a big smile on his face. He handed me a bottle of beer.

"I owe you an apology, doll. I was so excited to finally have you in my bed, and have sex with you, I guess I was in too much of a rush, and that couldn't have been good for you. Next time we will take it slow, and I promise you will enjoy yourself. Promise!!"

I couldn't even consider a "next time." I had to admit, though, that Ernie did sound sincere, and the look in his eyes, was so sweet, so pleading.

"I'm okay, Ern. Do you mind if I don't finish this beer and you can take me home now?"

"Please believe me, that I am truly sorry," Ernie said and then grabbed his car keys.

"Let's forget about it," I sighed.

Once I was home and in my room. I took my diary from its hiding place and wrote as fast as I could. I wanted to get it all down while my feelings (and body parts) were still raw.

"Dear Diary.

"Today I lost my virginity, and I am feeling so mixed up inside. I had I fantasized so long about this day, and it was NOTHING like I thought it would be. I thought it would be unforgettable, romantic, and so full of love!

"It was over before it barely started! No kisses or sweet sayings before we got going, just sex, and that was it!

"I know it wasn't the way Ernie wanted it either, and he did apologize, and was so very sorry. He promised it won't be like that ever again. I hope he means it.

"I do care about him. Maybe I even love him? Not sure.

"Goodnight Diary, I hope my next entry will be a lot happier."

Ernie kept his promise, and the sex was better the next time, not great, but a lot better. I knew he cared about me, and he kept telling me how much he loved me.

Things improved between us, and one day out of the blue, Ernie asked me to move in with him! I wasn't expecting his offer and didn't know how to answer.

Yes, I was secure living at home with Mom. We loved each other, but she treated me differently than how she had cared for me in my happy childhood. *Maybe it was all a part of growing up?*

Now, it was always, "Where have you been?" "Do you realize how late it was last night?" "When are you going to get a better job, and make something of yourself?"

Mom used to praise me when I was a child. She had made me feel so loved and appreciated; now it seemed all she could do was criticize me. I felt she was disappointed with me. Was it because I didn't have a better job? Was it because she didn't like, (or approve of Ernie)?

Seeing her unhappy with me, made me feel uncomfortable every time we were together.

The worse it got with Mom, the more I considered Ernie's offer.

We could clean his place up together, make it decent and livable for the two of us. Also, it would be great to have someone praising me, instead of always finding fault.

I finally told Ernie "Yes, let's do it. It will be fun." I hoped as I said it, I wasn't making a huge mistake.

The following week, I told my mom I was moving out. She was terribly hurt and wanted to know why. Mom's eyes filled with tears. Her hands trembled. The first question she rattled off was: "What have I done to upset you?"

I lied and told her "Ernie and I have fallen in love, and we want to be together. It's nothing you did."

She stood there listening, and the silence when one of us wasn't talking was deafening.

I rushed on, "You know how much I want to write and become an author. Well, Ernie is going to make that happen. He has a friend who's an editor, and he's going to read my work. He will help me get me published! Isn't that wonderful?" I said with a most triumphant tone. I'd really made it all up. Ernie had once said that he knew an editor, or publisher or something, I wasn't sure which. Still, I told myself it was true.

"No, it's NOT wonderful! What, does he have, a magic wand? Writing is hard, Madeline. I didn't want to tell you, but you were never that good at it. Now you need to know. You can't depend on writing to support you. Not unless you get a whole lot better."

Mom wailed out loud then and tried to hide her shaking hands by balling them into fists. "I'm sorry. I had to tell you that." She turned and walked slowly down the hall to her room.

I pulled my suitcase from the back of the closet and put my boom box in first. I would be lost without my music. Next, I packed my diary. If I forgot that, well, I couldn't even go there in my mind ... Let's just say Mom would have a cow if she ever found it and READ it! Like totally! I packed the few clothes I had. Two dresses. The blue jersey one that I wore constantly, and the beige one. That was it. I had a few sweaters, skirts, jeans, and not much else.

When I finished packing and came out of my room, I noticed Mom's door was closed. I hollered through the door. "I'm leaving now, Mom. Will you come out and say goodbye?"

I waited for a minute or so in the dead quiet. The door did not open. Finally, I said, "I'll call you, Mom. Take care of yourself. I love you."

Then I walked out the front door, carrying along with my suitcase a sense of freedom in my heart, that I had never felt before.

Ernie was waiting in his car at the curb. He flashed me a huge grin.

But, it didn't dawn on him to get his rump out of the driver's seat and help with my suitcase.

Oh well, he loves me.

"I can't believe I'm going to have you all to myself. We are going to be the hottest couple!" he said.

Ernie's car radio blared so loud; I didn't even attempt
to comment.

U2 crooned "With or Without You." I wasn't paying attention to
the song, or the words, but Ernie turned the volume down, then
looked at me and said "Baby, there will NEVER be a without
you! NEVER!"

Chapter Eight
MADELINE

May 1984

When we got to his place — "our" place — I looked around the messy apartment. I shouldn't have been surprised that nothing had changed in anticipation of my arrival. Ernie hadn't done a thing to clean the place up to welcome me.

No, I should have known that wouldn't even dawn on him. I'm sure he thought it looked fine as it was.

I looked in the refrigerator, and it was just as I expected. Filthy dirty, and not much in there, except a couple six packs of beer. Oh yes, and a carton of milk, and even with the cap on the carton, I could smell that it was sour!

I decided that would have to be the first "clean up job" for both of us. I wanted that accomplished before we went shopping for some "real" food!

Next, I went to the closet in the bedroom. Not many of clothes of Ernie's hanging in there. A pile of dirty clothes on the floor! AND ... no hangers for me to hang my stuff!

I figured the bathroom would be a disaster, too, as it had always been, and I was right! The bathtub had mold and grime all over it, and the shower was grimy, too! *Gross!*

We would need to buy a huge amount of cleaning items and do our best.

How could Ernie live like this?

"Ernie, what do you say we clean this place up a little? With the two of us working at it, we can have it ship-shape in no time."

Ernie turned, and looked at me, genuine surprise on his face. "Well," he spoke slowly. "If that's what you want to do, sweets. I mean ... " His eyes scanned the room. "I think it's fine the way it is."

"Please don't be offended." I moved to him and placed my hand on his arm. He stared at me, as I said, "I'm just used to having everything neat and clean. It's uh ... the way I kept my room," I said, stammering. "I would like it that way here, too. You understand, don't you?"

"Also," I dared to continue, "I think we should go shopping maybe for some new bed pillows. That would be nice. And some throw pillows for the couch?"

Ernie had the most darling twisted smile on his face, and I kissed the edge of his mouth. His expression softened under my lips. "Aw, don't go and make this place all cutesy on me now," he said.

I smiled sweetly into his eyes. "I'm not," I pouted just the slightest bit. "A few tweaks here and there, and that's it. I promise!"

Ernie laughed and smacked me on the behind. All was smoothed out, and we had some really awesome days in the beginning.

We did go shopping, and we did clean the place up! Also, we bought groceries — healthy food, at last.

Sure, Ernie was a little thoughtless at times, but I knew it wasn't intentional. And it was nothing new. He had a few ragged edges needing smoothing. Especially, in bed. He was always so excited and in such a hurry!

The sex was, for the most part, good and energetic. I tried to think only of how much Ernie loved me. *That was all that really mattered, right?*

One day when we were hanging around the apartment, I got all excited talking about my dream of being a writer. I had some awesome stories to tell inside me. He had mentioned his buddy, who was in the business and who could help me, and that day, he brought him up again.

Ernie flashed his signature toothy grin and said, "Believe it or not, ol' Ern's gonna come through for you." My eyes popped open as he continued.

"Babe, I will contact my bud this week, I swear. He'll hook you up with the right people, then boom!" He clapped his hands together, laughing when I jumped. Then he leaned in close, picked up my chin, kissed me and said, "Let's get you published!"

I wondered how he had connections in the publishing world for the second time as I watched Ern practically puffing out his chest.

How could the automotive and publishing world be connected anyway?

Ernie was the top mechanic at the largest automotive establishment in town. He made good money, and I knew he was good at fixing motors. "Anything mechanical, ol' Ern can fix it," he loved saying as he waved his hands. But every time I saw his hands, I tried to ignore the dark grease under his nails. I knew it was futile ever to think he could get rid of that.

At that moment, grease or not, my thoughts could only spin with the delicious possibility of becoming a published author!

Ernie shook me gently from my daydream. "A published author. The real deal. How does that sound, Maddie?"

"Fantastic." My hopes twirled all over the place again.

After that, I worked like crazy, writing during every available moment. My job was drudgery, and I merely tolerated it.

One day, I will trash this boring nine to five, and get on with my "real" life.

It wasn't long before I learned my mother, as cruel as she had been in telling me that I wasn't any good at writing, might have been right!

Finding the words didn't come easily. I had all these ideas, but I couldn't seem to get the right words on the paper. I didn't fantasize about the writing as much as I did about being famous and what living like a genuine author would mean to me. Still, I tried so hard to create these beautiful pieces.

I needed to come up with ideas. *What would constitute a great story? What kind of characters would readers enjoy?* I didn't have a clue. The little phrases in the greeting cards wouldn't be of any help.

Ernie kept cheering me on and telling me what a good writer I was, and so did the editor. It was exactly what I needed to hear, to keep going with enthusiasm. I couldn't thank Ernie enough, so I showed him every chance I got … in and out of bed.

Chapter Nine
ERNIE

May 1984

"Listen, hon; you have to believe me. You are a great writer and with this editor's help ... And by the way, I hooked you up with him. Don't forget that. If you keep plugging away, writing new stuff, you will finally succeed. I just know it, babe. You're talented. I can't wait to see what you turn out next."

Maddie shot me a skeptical look, but I could see she was desperate to believe what I said.

"Oh Ernie, do you think I have a chance of being published? I will work so hard, I promise."

The look on her face was so sincere; it broke my heart. It was so great having her around. And my feelings toward her were getting deeper. She wasn't a bad cook, and the dumpy apartment had never looked so good or been so clean.

I wished the sex was more exciting. I tried to teach her some new techniques, and positions, but she had little interest in that. She was always willing. I think in her mind, sex was an expression of how much I love her.

I guess I might be falling in love. First time for everything.

I was going to ask her to do a huge favor for me. I was sure she would when I reminded her of what I have been doing for her.

The editor thinks her writing is lousy, too. I am paying him a small amount of dough and giving him free service on his car, to keep him from telling her otherwise. Every time she writes something new, she wants me to sit with her on the couch, while she reads to me. I can hardly keep a straight face as I tell her how good it is, and that she keeps getting better and better. *How the hell can she think she is talented?* Beats me. I guess when you want something badly enough, you can talk yourself into believing anything.

When I was growing up, I tried to convince myself that I could be as good at sports as my older brother, Eddie.

Sure, he was bigger than me and far better looking, but I tried so hard to make my mom and dad as proud of me, as they were of Eddie.

He was way smarter in school, and he had awesome grades every year. Eddie was tops in everything. My parents never let an opportunity go by, without pointing that out to me, and anyone else they could corner and rave to.

Sure, I was sick of listening to all that praise for my brother, and I did try to do better in school, and in sports.

Then, I finally had to admit it. Eddie had it all over me, and no matter how hard I tried, I couldn't match him in ANYTHING!! It's not a great feeling to know you are second in your family favorites.

Eddie didn't have any problem with the girlfriend situation either. He always hooked up with the prettiest girls. The girls any guy would love to date! They all fell for Eddie!

At least I'd learned I was pretty good with machinery. I could repair my mom's vacuum and other appliances around the house. Mom thought this was cool, and I was very happy to receive some praise from her.

I'd finally found my niche. Maybe I would be some famous mechanic, or I might invent a new brilliant machine, that no one had ever thought of? I was willing to work hard to fulfill my high hopes and dreams.

Chapter Ten
MADELINE

Late May – Early June 1984

One night, after making love, Ernie said, "Sweets, I want you to do a favor for me."

"Oh, Ern, I would do just about anything for you. You know that." I told him.

"There's this guy. His name is Cliff. We used to be friends a long time ago, and then he double-crossed me with a gal I was crazy about at the time."

"Oh, Ern honey, I am so sorry. What happened?"

"Well, I felt like I wasn't getting to first base with this gal, and I really wanted her to like me. This is so crazy, I know, but I asked Cliff if he would take her out, with the sole purpose of 'piping' me up to her. You know, make me sound like a movie star or whatever."

Ernie had a wild intensity in his eyes as he talked, and I sat back and studied him. I had never seen him like this. *Why did he still care about another girl anyway?*

He rambled on, telling me he had given Cliff Yvonne's number and then they had started dating.

"I was such a damn fool ever to think a crazy scheme like that would work. How did I tolerate the two of them together, even at a restaurant, never mind HAVING SEX!!!!"

Ernie paused to catch his breath, then picked up telling the story.

"Yvonne started to fall for HIM!! That bastard! It was the end of our friendship of course. Well, I *knew* it was the end, even if Cliff thought we could ever be friends again. I didn't know if I would ever get over it. But, I met you, and Yvonne is nothing more to me now than a distant memory. Baby, you are everything to me that matters. But I feel like I should even the score somehow."

Ernie sat forward and put his hands together like he was praying. He closed his eyes, and wrinkled up his mouth, in a very sad way.

"I couldn't look at his cheating face again," he mumbled.

He sat back in the chair and tried to compose himself. *Was he going to cry?*

"So, Maddie, sweetie," He found his voice again, "I was thinking we could do the old switcheroo. You know, you pretend to care about Cliff. He'll fall for you hard. Any guy would."

I pressed my lips together and forced myself to listen without interrupting.

"Then when he is truly hooked, we will pull the rug out from under him, and he'll know how much it hurts when someone plays with your life, and your feelings."

The fire in Ernie's eyes had died down. "It will all be a setup." Then he looked at me, and for a minute I suspected he had forgotten I was there.

"Isn't this idea the perfect payback?"

My voice quivered as I answered him, "Ernie," I sighed. "Wow, that sounds awful. You want to play with his feelings that hard? You're purposely hurting him."

"That's the whole idea. Let him find out how bad life can get when your friend lies their ass off."

Well, it was a terrible and insane idea. It was also mean. "It sounds dangerous," I hedged. "I'm not sure I can do it."

When Ernie spoke next, his voice held a snide edge. "Sure, you can, my talented 'writer-to-be.' You can do anything you want for me, just like I can do ... or not do ... anything I want for you."

I'm just beginning to feel comfortable in our relationship, and now he wants to take it all away?

What he was proposing was a form of blackmail, and I couldn't believe Ernie would ever pit my dream of becoming a writer and helping me achieve that, to make me enter into some sick, vengeful plan. *Yes, Ernie was that hell-bent on revenge.*

It broke my heart and scared me to death! I saw a new side of Ernie, and I didn't like it.

Later, when I was alone, I pulled my diary out, and began writing:

"Dear Diary,

"Ernie is plotting the most despicable plan, and it involves me! It is all just a sick idea of revenge, to get back at a friend that had betrayed him, years ago.

"I protested, but that was when he reminded me what a great favor he is doing for me, hooking me up with an editor. Such a rotten choice that I have no way out of!"

What else could I do, but go along with his plans?

We plotted out the party where I would meet Cliff at our apartment. I had protested and made suggestions of giving up on such a terrible intention. Ernie wouldn't budge.

I pulled out all the stops when I got dressed and styled my hair. The evening of the party, Ernie's eyes raked over my figure, and he gave a low wolf whistle when I walked into the room. I didn't say a word.

"You look incredibly gorgeous, Maddie. Cliff doesn't have a chance in hell. He will be an instant goner!" Ernie's voice was jubilant!

When Cliff arrived at the party, I knew he found me attractive the moment he spotted me. After that, it was easy, even though I had a sick pit in my stomach.

I didn't like playing the terrible game, and I resented Ernie for asking me to play a part.

Cliff seemed like a decent guy, and yes, rather shy in the dating game. It was all going to be a disaster. I couldn't muster up much respect for myself or Ernie!

Cliff and I started dating, as was the plan.

The more time I spent with him, the better I liked him. I wasn't sure in the beginning if the "dates" would ever to lead to sex. Looking back, I can see it was inevitable! We seemed so suited to each other.

I was getting good at dodging Ernie and his questions. He worked opposite hours from me, so we hadn't ever spent a huge amount of time together. Either one or both of us always seemed to be at our jobs. It wasn't hard to lose myself in Clifford and our new relationship.

One night, when I was alone in the apartment, I answered the phone, knowing it was Ernie. He was working his usual night shift. He had been trying to track me down, and I had avoided him as much as possible.

"Hello, Ernie sweetheart," I cooed. "I have missed you more than you could ever know."

"You think you have missed me?" Ernie growled. "I am going out of my mind, Maddie. This has got to stop! I can't stand it anymore! And why aren't you ever home anymore? Whenever I finish my shift, and finally get home, feeling so anxious to see you, you aren't there! I am really getting sick of this."

"Ernie, this was your idea, remember? You're the one who dreamed up this nightmare in the first place." I twirled the phone cord as I tried to placate him. I was getting tired of his attitude more often. I was allowed to have a life after all; even though the life Ernie had created for me wasn't what I had planned, it wasn't all bad. Cliff was as great a guy as any girl could ever want. I certainly was not miserable.

"I know," Ernie said. "but it is more than I can stomach. We have to call it off. What the hell is going on anyway?"

I panicked.

"Everything is going as you planned, Ernie, and you will have your revenge, you so desperately wanted. Hope you're happy!"

Not only was the crazy plan that Ernie concocted falling apart, I was so hurt that Ernie would talk to me that way. I thought he liked that I'd asked for his approval with my writing, and then he had come up with his rotten scheme.

I guess what I had thought before about us, wasn't true. All he ever did want from me was the sex. Look where that had gotten me!

I called my mom. "How are you doing?" I asked her. "How are you feeling? Boy, I sure have been missing you and living in my own room at home. What would you think of me moving back home? Are you missing me, too?"

"No, Madeline, you are not invited to move back home. I warned you this would happen. I knew you would be unhappy living with Ernie, but you wouldn't listen to me." I couldn't believe what I heard as I gripped the phone. "Ernie never had your best interests in mind, only his own. Why couldn't you see that? I am sorry that you are unhappy, but this is the choice you made, and now you have to live with it."

Hearing her made me understand how many mistakes I had made. *Now, what was I to do, when nobody, not even my mother wanted me?*

I wasn't so happy either. I was playing an evil part in a twisted play. I felt sick to my stomach almost every morning, and that's when I checked the calendar and realized I had MISSED MY PERIOD!!!

Oh, please God, please, don't let me be pregnant. It would be a disaster for everyone. I wasn't even sure which one was the father.

I couldn't imagine Ernie wanting to start a family, and I didn't think he'd had anything like that in mind when he'd asked me to move in with him. *He would be a good provider, and a fun and loving dad, but that would mean, what? Getting married? Live with Ernie the rest of my life?!*

How would Cliff feel about my being pregnant? I started secretly hoping that Cliff would be the father. And I could picture our life together. Cliff, the doctor, providing for us, our beautiful home, wonderful vacations ... *But ... maybe Cliff wouldn't welcome a baby either?*

We had never talked about having a family or even getting married.

I know Cliff cares about me, maybe even loves me. Would he still love me if he ever found out about what Ernie and I were up to?

I doubted it.

It was bound to come out. Why hadn't I seen that in the beginning?

Would Cliff put all of that aside, because of the idea of having a baby? Or, maybe he would care a lot less about me!?

I thought he might dump me.

Maybe it was too soon to tell if I was pregnant if I took a test, but I had to try.

I came back from the drugstore with the test, and my hands shook when I tore the wrapper off.

My entire life could be changing, and maybe not for the better! It seemed hours before the test finished.

When it came up "negative," I was so relieved.

Then, it dawned on me that maybe it WAS too soon, and the results wouldn't be accurate! Guess I had to wait a little longer. I prayed my heart out in the meantime.

After another 10 anxious, horrible days, I FINALLY got my period.

Chapter Eleven
ERNIE

July – August 1984

I changed the phone from my left ear to my right. My heart raced. My stomach was a mess, as it had been for the last couple of months. *Why was Maddie so sassy?* She hadn't talked to me that way before. I couldn't shake the feeling that she wanted to get off the phone. *What the hell is going on with her?* I wasn't sure I wanted to know the answer.

"Why are we pulling the plug so early?" Maddie asked. "I know Cliff has fallen for me, as we had hoped. Isn't that what you wanted? I have to admit, though, there is a bit of a problem," Madeline said cautiously, her voice cracking.

"What kind of problem?" I practically snarled through the phone. "Maddie, what the hell … You are killing me here!"

"I don't know quite how to say this, Ernie, and I know we certainly didn't plan on this happening, but …"

"Spit it out, Maddie. Goddamn it!"

"I am kind of starting to have, you know, feelings for Cliff, too. I mean, not the way I feel about you, Ernie ... but I sure do enjoy being with him."

"What?? Are you insane? I cannot believe this!"

"I didn't plan on it, Ernie. This was your screwed-up plan to get back at Cliff. I just went along with it to please you," Maddie said rather irritably.

She's annoyed with ME?

"Well, you sure aren't pleasing me now. Have you lost your mind? You think you're falling for that jerk?"

I heard Maddie, start talking again, but at the same time, I couldn't understand the words. *How had the same damn situation happened again to me? What the hell was wrong with me?*

"I-I don't know." She went on, "We do have a good time together, and the sex is outstanding, and I ... " Maddie broke off, her voice a whisper.

"Spare me the details, for God's sake. How much more of this crap do you think I can take?"

"It's just that Cliff is so sweet. Don't be mad, Ern. I can't help it."

"I'm hanging up. Don't bother calling me. I need some air. Some *clean* air."

I slammed the receiver down as hard as I could. It sounded like the phone cracked. I didn't care. I ran my fingers through my hair crazily. Then I grabbed my jacket and hurried out the door. I was just about finished for the day with my job, and I figured "what the hell?" I needed to get out of there more than I needed the couple extra bucks.

Tiny's bar was right down the street. It was a good place to sit, drink and decide what to do next. All I could think was *that bitch. After all we meant to each other … she pulls this crap?*

I found an empty seat at the bar. As usual, Cyndi crooned "Time After Time." Remarkable that Tiny never tired of the same tune. It made me want to punch the wall.

Tiny swaggered over as much as an obese man can, and asked, "What'll it be?"

I couldn't get out the words fast enough. "Double Jack. Thanks."

How many double Jacks would it take to stop the tremor in my hands? Would there ever be enough to dull the pain?

I loved and hated Madeline all at once.

The drinks went down fast. "I should have known better. Cliff was always more of a ladies' man than I could ever be. But for Maddie to give up on us, and what we had going … unreal!" I realized I had spoken out loud as I sat by myself at the bar and then I quickly noted I didn't care. I didn't care much about anything, except maybe getting drunk!

I stayed rooted to the spot for a couple of hours, downing far too many shots. When I looked down the length of the bar with glassy eyes, I could have sworn there was Annie also sitting alone.

What the hell is she doing here?

Our eyes met, and Annie picked up her drink and hustled over to my side.

"Cliff and I just finished a doozy of a job, and I needed to stop in for a short libation before heading home," Annie said, her voice high with excitement.

"Cliff's still at the morgue?"

"I guess so," Annie said. "He told me to skedaddle. Said he didn't need me for the clean-up. He's such a great guy."

That was the last thing I wanted to hear. I never wanted to hear it ever, but *please, GOD not now!* My rage at Cliff was at an all-time high, and it was only made worse with the knowledge that Cliff wasn't the antagonist, I was!

As much as I had blamed Maddie, I had taken the risk. But Cliff had still screwed me a second time, and that was too much!

"I usually meet my sister here once a week, but she went home to Seattle to visit our folks. So, I'm here by my lonesome," said Annie. "Well, not my lonesome anymore, right?"

Annie's red hair shone in the fluorescent lights, and she flashed her dimples a lot as we talked. *She's not a bad looking gal. Wonder why Cliff never went after her?*

"Yeah right," I grumbled in response to Annie's comment. *Was Annie coming on to me? I was in no mood for romance!*

"Guess I had better hit the road myself while I can still walk." I put down a few bills to cover my tab. "See ya."

"Bye," Annie said, as she watched me turn toward the door. Her dimples were nowhere to be seen.

I fished for my keys and made my way to the parking lot behind Tiny's. It was long damn walk all of a sudden. I knew I shouldn't get behind the wheel, but I did anyway.

Then I drove directly to the morgue. The lights glowed inside the front door. That meant people were still in the building. I got out of the car and climbed the steps to the building. When I tried the door, it was locked.

I wove my way back down the steps and to the car, thinking, *I'll wait here until the bastard comes out. The element of surprise!*

Chapter Twelve
MADELINE

August 1984

I sat by the phone for an hour, feeling lousy about everything.

"Ernie should never have tried to hurt Cliff the way Cliff had hurt him all those years ago. Such a shame. Now everyone loses," I said to the empty air.

I'd thought the idea was crazy from the beginning. *And I never should have agreed to it.* Dabbing my eyes with a tissue, a huge knot formed in my stomach.

"Maybe I should call Cliff and tell him the whole story? I know he is in love with me. This will really hurt."

Yeah, I was still talking out loud to no one, my voice thready in my ears.

Chapter Thirteen
CLIFFORD

August 1984

It was one of those late nights. I was inside the morgue finishing up after assisting with the male victim of a random drive-by shooting. *Such a senseless, violent and needless death,* I thought as I covered the victim and then rolled the gurney to the nearest empty drawer. I shoved the body inside.

I pulled off my gloves and gown, then threw them in the biohazard waste container.

Glad to have that over with. Such a young kid.

I tried hard to stay detached in my work, but kids were always the toughest. They were the worst cases of all. "Time to get the hell out of here. Very long day, not one of the best, that's for sure," I mumbled, half out loud.

I finished the rest of the cleaning, then yanked my coat on, turned out the lights and stepped outside. It was drizzling so I pulled my collar up around my face.

Suddenly, a figure stepped in front of me.

What the hell?

"Big surprise, Cliff, but not as big a surprise as I have in store for you," wheezed Ernie.

Ernie tried to grab my collar but missed, as he swayed in the misty night.

"Ern, what are you doing? How much have you had to drink? What's going on?"

"I can't wait to tell you 'what's going on,' as you put it. You stupid, asshole," Ernie yelled. He weaved on his feet again, his rank breath in my face once more. "You are in for a really big surprise. You won't like it, but it serves you right, you shit."

"Ern, what the hell are you talking about? What is the matter with you?" I hollered, as my voice rose higher and higher.

"It was a setup. A joke. Anything to make you look like the jerk that you are," Ernie growled still staggering around the steps and too close to my face. The steps were concrete, with cracks, and chips missing on the edges. I thought for sure, Ernie would stumble and fall.

"What joke? What set up? Ernie, you're not making any sense."

"Madeline, Dumbass! She is *my* girl. Mine. Get it? We planned all this, so you would fall for her and then she would dump you. Just the way Yvonne dumped me. How do you like it so far? How does it feel? You were easy. Such a jerk."

My head hurt ferociously, and it got worse the more Ernie talked. I fought through a mental fog to hear the rest of what he had to say.

"So, get over it. The party's over. You won't be seeing Maddie anymore because I will be the one she crawls on the sheets with. Oh, I feel so much better now," Ernie said, lurching forward as if he might fall.

I grabbed him, and Ernie swatted my hands. "You get away from me. I hope I never have to see your sorry mug again. Have a nice life. I know I will, with Madeline. Goodbye!"

Ernie wobbled down the steps and across the street to his car. I stood there glued to the wet pavement. My brain couldn't or wouldn't process what Ernie had just told me. I thought of Madeline. *Goddammit, I knew she loved me! Me! Cliff Wilson!*

"Ernie's out of his head. Madeline will call as soon as I get home. Hell, we'll have a good laugh over Ernie being so smashed and talking like a lunatic." My mind and my insides begged for the words I spoke to be true.

I called Madeline on her cell (which she finally had given me) as soon as I walked in the door. I bypassed the chit-chat and blurted, "Maddie, I just ran into Ern, and he told me the most bizarre story. It can't be true! Please tell me it's a crock of bullshit!"

There was no answer for a minute, only a long, heavy silence.

Then Maddie's voice split the air. It was tight and hoarse. "What kind of things?"

I told her everything that Ernie had said, that she was *his* girl, that it was a set-up.

"Isn't that the most ludicrous story you have ever heard?" I asked her. I tried to laugh, but it sounded more like a sob. I needed her answer but didn't know if I could handle it. I silently prayed it was all a joke on Ern's part. As I tried to puzzle out the sick mystery, I thought my head would burst open. "Maddie! Answer me, damn it! I am dying over here!"

No words came through the end of the phone. The silence was longer this time. I thought I was going to be sick. I couldn't stop drumming my fingers on the desk. Sweat ran down my back and under my arms. I couldn't decide if I should throw something or scream my lungs out.

"Maddie, answer me! Is any of this true? It's all a joke, right? Ern's trying to get my goat, scare the hell out of me?"

She didn't say a word. The tears were going to come no matter what I did.

Finally, "Yes, it's true." Her small, weak voice bled through the line. "I am so sorry. It was Ernie's idea. I didn't want to go along with it. You have to believe me. He insisted, said you needed a payback for ruining his relationship with Yvonne."

Was she crying, too?

"I told him he was childish, but he wouldn't give up."

I couldn't grasp what she'd said.

"I am so sorry, Cliff. More sorry than you will ever know. I should have never gone along with it. And it was all in the name of revenge."

Madness was all I could think.

Her voice again. "Please, forgive me, please."

Then the worst part of the whole thing hit me. I did believe her. She had been sucked in, but the fact remained, she'd done it anyway. *Had she ever really loved me?*

It was my turn to be quiet while my face flushed hot and sweaty. I had the worst ache in my throat.

"Cliff, can you ever forgive me? I love you! I love both of you," she sobbed. "I know that sounds crazy, and right now, I feel like I am crazy! I hate myself for hurting you. I always will! Please, Cliff, say you understand, that you'll forgive me."

I didn't say anything. There was nothing but the sound of her breathing, and then she said, "I will never lie to you again."

My eye twitched amid the rumblings of a horrendous head-ache. I couldn't trust myself to say anything that would even be coherent. So, I hung up. I didn't know if Madeline was still talking and I didn't care.

She didn't call back.

What was there left to say?

I walked around the apartment, unsure what to do. Shatter all the plates? Knock the furniture over? Scream? Throw a bunch of shit around? What good would any of that do?

This can't be happening.

It was the first time in my life I had ever been crazy about a gal, and the feelings were mutual. And, boy was it heaven. But that was the keyword, now … *WAS.*

Suddenly, I felt sick. Then I wondered h*ow many painkillers can I take?* I didn't care if I overdosed. Still, I took a couple. The headache had gripped me off and on like a vice. But I finally did get worn out enough to hit the sack. Walking around in circles didn't help.

Sleep wasn't on the agenda even though I tried. I swallowed several aspirins, too, hoping to lessen the misery in my head. It didn't do a damn thing. I laid in bed, rolling around and clutching my temples. My mind raced, and the tension kept climbing until I thought my brain would explode.

I lumbered out of bed, filled the ice pack and shoved it on my aching head. I flipped on the TV, hoping the drone of what-ever the hell was on would put me to sleep. I hated *The Dukes of Hazard,* but that night I didn't give a shit. I wasn't paying atten-tion, and any distraction was welcome.

I think I dozed a little, maybe I even slept. I had dreams of Madeline and the first time we met. I awoke with my head pounding and my eyelid fluttering.

Good God, I thought I had made points with Maddie at Ernie's party.

He had claimed he didn't even know her. At last, I'd untangled all the mystery, like why Maddie had said she could never introduce me to any of her friends.

It was all starting to fit. *How could they?* I hated both of them, and I hated myself, too, for being such a fool. *Why hadn't I been able to see through it?* I knew why.

I was in love.

Shit!! No wonder she hadn't let me into her apartment. *She was living with Ernie, for God's sake! UNBELIEVABLE!!!*

Her "friend," who lived with her was Ernie! They'd covered their tracks. I had to give them that! I hadn't once suspected the truth.

But there had to be payback. Now, it would be MY turn! How extreme, I hadn't decided, but I would give my own plan a lot of long and careful thought. I was devastated! I was furious! I was hurting and in such agonizing pain.

The final epiphany I had before dropping off to sleep near the morning hours was: *They deserve each other.*

Chapter Fourteen

MADELINE

August 1984

Cliff slammed the phone down in my ear so hard, letting me know how angry he was!

Suddenly my vision became blurred. I knew I was going to be sick. And I was!

I could barely see my way to the bathroom, and the toilet. In fact, I did miss the bowl, not completely, but still, I made a horrible mess. Vomit was everywhere around the bowl.

I sat on the bathroom floor, feeling sicker than I ever had. *Was I having a panic attack?* I thought that must be it.

I was too sick to clean the floor, so, I slowly made my way to the bed. The room was spinning. I closed my eyes and felt I was going to be sick again, and I was! I had to be careful not to slip in the puddle I had made. I made my way back from the bathroom again, trying to ignore how awful the room smelled.

I wanted to die. I was miserable. I despised myself, and Ernie. I had been such a dope to be sucked into Ernie's insane idea.

He'd claimed he had a publisher that would be interested in my writing. What a load of shit that was! *He is a liar and a blackmailer! He is blackmailing me with that promise. Yes, I HATE him. How could Ernie lie to me and use me?* I was a puppet. *I hate myself more!* I'd let my silly dreams get in the way of reality. I seemed to do that a lot. Where had that ever gotten me? NOWHERE!!

In my heart and mind, I knew I wasn't that good at writing. Yeah, one teacher in grade school had praised some silly poem I had written, and that had led me to believe I had talent. I'd wanted so badly to believe it; I had convinced myself it was true.

Hadn't my mom almost laughed out loud when I'd told her Ernie had an editor that would get me published?

I had been so smug about it, telling myself, *well, I'll show her.*

Now, who'd had the last laugh? Mom and I hadn't been in touch very much lately. My fault, though I know, she has not quite forgiven me for moving out. And … in with Ernie of all people.

Can't blame her. She had a bad experience with my dad and wanted me to be with someone who would take care of me.

I think I finally dozed a little. Then I had dreams of Cliff, of when we were together, and so happy. In the dream, it didn't get to the part where I was lying to him and betraying his love and trust.

I woke up and thought I felt a little better, but I wasn't sure. My vision had improved, but whenever I thought about what I had done, I felt like I would be sick again.

After throwing up for the third time, I staggered to the kitchen, advising myself to eat some crackers, or maybe have a soda, or carbonated drink.

The whole situation was absurd, and I knew it, but I was in love with both Clifford and Ernie. *Whoever had heard of such a goofy thing? A girl can't love two guys at the same time, can she? But I was doing it.*

I knew Ernie wasn't the man of my dreams, but he was good to me, and we did have some memorable and loving times.

Was that love?

Then there was Cliff.

He was the sweetest, most caring guy in the world. He was educated and so handsome and considerate of my feelings. I did believe they both loved me. They had each showed it in very genuine ways. Ernie, through his clumsy manner of trying to take care of me, and Clifford through every little gesture he made to show I mattered.

Now what?

Probably they both despise me, and I hate me, too. I've lost them.

I crawled back into bed and pulled the blankets up to my tear-soaked chin.

My mind seesawed back and forth between the two men in my life.

Ernie was kind, steady and funny. He cheered me up whenever my feelings were in the dumpster. He made me feel secure, and I found myself depending on him more and more.

I thought we were getting closer to heading down the aisle, too.

Ernie's voice echoed in my mind: "That lousy shit was anything but a friend. If he had stuck a knife in me, he couldn't have hurt me more."

After much coaxing and pleading, I'd finally caved.

What a terrible mistake I will regret for the rest of my life.

Chapter Fifteen
CLIFFORD

August – September 1984

My headaches returned with a vengeance! My eyesight blurred, as the throbbing continued like the beating of a thousand bongo drums.

The pain in my heart tormented me even more. My thoughts soured as I fought through the sheer agony ripping through every cell.

"What a lousy bitch she turned out to be." I gripped my head in my hands, wishing I could reach inside and yank out the pulsing pain.

"She doesn't deserve to be happy with or without me. She doesn't deserve to live!"

The seed of evil germinated in my tortured head. Once it took root, I couldn't let it go.

Could I go that far?

How would I take care of business?

How COULD I do this?

It was time for some research because I needed the reassurance I could get away with it.

The headaches slowed down. The plan for payback made me feel better. It was cold and heartless, and I could sense that on a superficial level, *but cold and heartless was who Madeline was,* I reasoned. *She obviously didn't have thoughts or feelings for anyone but herself.*

Revenge consumed me. *What method will I use to wipe the bitch off the planet? A gun? It was too common. Besides, where would I get a gun?*

Strangulation? I didn't know if I had the strength, and if not, I would botch the job.

Poison? Now, that was an "aha" I decided. And I had easier access to poison, considering my medical degree. *What poison? When? How?*

I went about my daily routine, but my mind stayed vigilant on killing Madeline. I hadn't been so focused on a goal since before I had met her … when I was immersed in school.

At times, I couldn't believe I was relishing the thought of murdering anyone, let alone the one person in the world who I'd loved with all my being.

No time for being a wuss now. You can and will do this. Guess Ernie won't be climbing on the sheets with Maddie after all.

Chapter Sixteen
ERNIE

September 1984

My old life meant nothing. I had no attachment to it anymore. I had lost Cliff as a friend for a second time, and more importantly, I'd lost Maddie.

What kind of a future did I have? A lousy job at a gas station. *Yeah, big deal, a mechanic.*

Nope, I would have to live with the fact that I was a loser. Guess I always had been, according to my mom and dad anyway.

Never could live up to my brother Eddie who had been an expert in EVERYTHING!

Eddie probably could have gotten into the movies if he wanted. No way, could I match him. I was reminded of our differences almost daily.

I loved Eddie but did resent feeling "less."

I knew then my scheme was a stupid idea!

Numbly, I pulled on my jacket and hit Tiny's for the second time that week. I told some of the story to Tiny but couldn't bring myself to share the whole thing. I was in too much pain.

What the hell? No one wants to see my face. I was gonna blow the town for good. Book a flight to Hawaii. Palm trees, hula dancers, beaches ... and lots of tropical drinks with those goofy umbrellas. It was the perfect prescription to take my mind off the hellish circumstances I'd made.

Then in the next second, I knew it was all stupid. I had to give it more thought before I decided to do anything. Whatever I did lately wasn't turning out the way I had planned.

Chapter Seventeen
MADELINE

September 1984

There was no point in keeping my job, so I quit.
I couldn't concentrate. I didn't get dressed every day, didn't eat.
Staying in bed was my refuge. I never thought I'd be back to that
level of surviving when I had lost my fiancé so many years ago.
Then my days and nights had been the same hell town as what
I was living.

My mind sank into a state of deep depression. The longer I shut
myself away from the world, seeing no one, the further I went
into my mind. Life held no promise anymore. I thought about
suicide all the time.

*I have plenty of sleeping pills in the medicine cabinet. How difficult
would it be to swallow the entire bottle and go to sleep ... forever?*

I wondered if I had the courage to do it. I wondered if I had the
courage not to do it.

Chapter Eighteen
CLIFFORD

October 1984

After researching different poisons, I found the perfect one for killing Madeline — Abrin.

I'd picked up a book on poisons and read: "Abrin is a yellowish-white powder that is derived from the seeds of the rosary pea, also called the jequirity pea. If ingested, the victim will develop symptoms as early as six hours later, but more likely won't for one to three days. There is no known test for Abrin, so the ME might not be able to determine the cause of death. The symptoms include shortness of breath, cough, chest pain, nausea and pulmonary edema (lungs full of water). The victim will literally drown in the water that collects within the lungs, suffer cardiac and respiratory failure and die."

Abrin could be found in abundance in Florida or other tropical areas. Anyone could obtain it as the seeds were used to make necklaces.

It would be smarter to drive to Florida, rather than fly, as there wouldn't be any proof I had ever been there.

So, I went to the bank, drew out enough cash to cover driving costs and the cost of the poison.

The next morning before dawn, I embarked on my journey. The trip went well and fortunately; I was not plagued by headaches.

As I drove, I blared music to keep my mind off the true purpose of my journey.

I took Route 75 all the way because it made for a long, easy drive.

When I arrived in Naples, I checked into a middle-class motel and paid cash for the room.

I slept for about four hours and then set out to find Abrin. First, I went to a market called Tin City in the center of the town and found all kind of artifacts and junk jewelry.

I looked around, and after a few wrong turns found a jewelry store with a bunch of cheap-looking stuff. Bracelets, rings, pins, and NECKLACES!

I zeroed in on a certain necklace that looked like the "stones" could be beads, thinking *maybe it could be THE ONE!!*

I asked the clerk, (who looked like she was on her last legs, and bored out of her mind, spending her days in such a dump) if the beads were from the rosary plant? She barely bothered to answer my question, muttering "No."

I asked next if she knew of anyone in the Tin City shops, or anywhere for that matter where I might find them.

*Did she know they were poisonous and what my intentions were?
I feel guilty already!*

Again, she didn't have a clue.

I did traipse around the rest of the shops and found nothing.
So many of the shops were selling those long maxi dresses, with
either palm trees or hibiscus flowers — all of them cheaply made.

I tried every jewelry shop, and came up empty, in each one.

Then, I went back to my car and thought about what to do next.

I doubted the beads would be in any other part of Florida.

But then I remembered reading that the beads, from the rosary
plant, could be found in tropical countries. *Where? South America.
Somewhere down there?* I felt sure that I could find them in Brazil.
That was one of the countries on the list.

I drove my car to the airport and parked in long-term parking
since I had no idea how far my search would take me.

I went inside the terminal and booked a flight to Brazil. It was as
good a place to check as any other. India was also on the list, but
that seemed a bit ridiculous to take a trip that far to locate the
beads! I was getting more anxious about ending the search and
completing my plan!

The flight went okay, except when the stewardess asked if I was
feeling okay.

"I'm fine," I answered. "Why do you ask?"

"You're very pale, and your eyes have a glassy look," she replied.

The nerve of her, I thought. *None of her or anyone else's business.*

She walked down the aisle with a slight shrug.

The trip to Brazil took over six hours.

Miraculously, I was able to sleep on the plane and was happy I could manage that. *All this legwork was wearing me out!*

When I arrived in Brazil, it was even more humid and hot than Florida! That was not going to slow me down. "I am here now, and I will find the beads." I was determined as I spoke the words aloud.

I did a little detective work and asked a few official looking people where I might find the rosary pea plant and the beads. It seemed everyone in and around the airport had "ears open."

A shabby guy approached me then, and said, "Mister, I can show you where to find the plant with the beads. It will cost you 200 dollars, but you will have what you are looking for. Pay in advance."

When he was talking, I realized his English was quite sketchy, but at least I could understand him.

"What is my guarantee that you will take me to the plant I am looking for?" I asked.

"No guarantee. Pay now."

I guessed he hadn't had a bath in weeks, or maybe months. His body odor confirmed it. He had a hideous grin, and when he smiled, two front teeth were missing. The rest of his teeth were stained yellow. He was some kind of derelict, or worse. I figured he was homeless, and I wondered what he would do with my 200 dollars.

I didn't smell too sweet either. I had on the same shirt I had worn on the drive down to Florida.

Add to that all the scouting around Florida in the humidity and the fact I hadn't changed when I boarded the plane either.

I was skeptical and fearful, but hell, I had come so far, and I was NOT going home empty-handed.

He led me to the side parking lot to an old rickety Jeep that had seen better days, as had he.

He started driving, (after I paid him.) and the roads got worse and more rutted as he drove.

We entered a dense forest, and I thought all my common sense had left me.

As we trekked deeper into the forest, I got panicky. *Maybe he's a murderer?*

He has my money, and no one knows where I am! He could kill me and leave my body here in this jungle!

Suddenly, he stopped the Jeep and got out. I followed him as he walked over to a bunch of odd plants.

He bent down and picked a branch from a particular plant then held the plant up for my inspection.

I couldn't believe it! The plant had several of the red and black beads all the way up and down the branch.

"Are you sure this is the plant I'm looking for?" I asked.

"Hey, Amigo, I told you I would find it for you, and this is it!"

BINGO!!

The beads did look like the ones in the picture, that I had researched in the book of poisons.

FINALLY!!!

I shook his gnarly hand and thanked him. As I did, I wondered if he knew they were poisonous, and maybe had given some thought as to why I wanted them, and how I would use them.

We piled into the Jeep again, and he warned me that it would be best to wrap the branch in a heavy box, or bag.

"Be sure not to break the beads open. They are full of poison." He handed me an old rag to cushion the branch, and of course, I was overly careful not to break any of the beads.

I figured I would buy a heavy bag at the airport.

We said our goodbyes as he dropped me off, and I was satisfied with finally ending my search.

I found a heavy bag at an airport shop. "Brazil" was printed all over the canvas.

Placing the branch in a bag that was much thicker than the rag made me feel a lot better.

I bought a ticket to Florida, with a short layover. I should have been wiped out, but I was so pumped up with my purchase, and up-coming plans I didn't feel the least bit tired.

The flight home featured another nosy stewardess inquiring about my health.

Do I look that bad? I feel pretty damn good!

I felt lucky also that I'd found an aisle seat.

The middle seat was empty, and I considered putting the bag on that seat. I was just trying to decide if that would be wise when an old woman came trudging down the aisle.

She gave me her best smile and asked if the center seat was taken.

I had a moment's thought that I should say yes, then thought, *heck, it won't kill me to have her sit here.*

"No, it is not taken. Let me help you with your bag," I said with a big grin.

"Well, aren't you just the nicest young man ever!" she exclaimed. *What a joke,* I thought. *She has no intuition.*

We were all buckled in our seats and took off almost immediately.

The next thing I knew, she reached into her bag and pulled out a sandwich. It smelled to high heaven of garlic, and other vile ingredients.

She started munching away, totally oblivious of the stench she was creating in the plane.

When she finally finished eating, she reached into her bag again to put the empty wrapper away.

And when she did that ... she FARTED!!

Holy God, if I'd had thought the plane had smelled bad before, this was soooo much worse! *I hope that is the end of the eating and her gas situation!* I thought. *Maybe she will fall asleep.* Thank the heavens, she did.

I was so happy to arrive back in Florida. My trip was all worth it!

The drive home from the airport went easily and quickly.

All that was on my mind was how good I was feeling, and how excellent I would feel when I gave Maddie what she deserved! *That awful bitch!*

Did she really think she could tromp all over a good guy like Cliff Wilson, and break his heart, all the while laughing it up on how she, and Ernie had pulled such a trick?

Did she think she could get away with that, and suffer no punishment? Was she mad?

I knew both she and Ernie were nut cases for sure!

I put the branch in the bottom drawer of my dresser next to some old shirts I never wore. It was as good a place as any.

I finally decided that I should probably get some sleep.

But as I lie there, I couldn't believe I still didn't feel that tired!

The next morning, I called Maddie, and a lie rolled out of my mouth without even thinking about it. I was setting our final date.

I told her that after thinking everything over, I could understand her position in trying to please Ernie. I went on to say, that I'd realized she was a pawn.

"How about meeting to see if we can piece our feelings back together? I have to admit, I can't stop thinking about you," I said, hoping I sounded sincere.

"Cliff, I cannot believe this is happening. I'm so miserable. I quit my job, haven't gone out at all. I see no one. I would be thrilled to see you! Do you think you could ever forgive me?"

I pictured how she would look on the other end of the phone and quickly had to shut down that thought. Let her wonder if we had a chance. Let her heart endure torture.

"When, Cliff? Just tell me when and where and I'll be there."

I told her it would be best to meet somewhere quiet where we could talk, but I had other reasons for needing the seclusion.

"Yes, Cliff. You decide," Maddie said eagerly.

I picked our favorite restaurant and told her to meet me at seven o'clock the next evening.

"You have to be the kindest, most forgiving man in the world," Madeline said in a pleading tone. "Thank you."

As I sat there listening to her voice, I felt lower than ever. She had hit me below the belt for the last time.

Kind, and forgiving Nope ... Hilarious is more like it!

"I'll be ready," Madeline said, and then we hung up.

Chapter Nineteen
MADELINE

November 1984

As soon as Cliff and I disconnected, I raced to the mirror and examined my reflection. *Would I be able to pull myself together enough with only one day?* I had a lot of work to do. Dark circles ringed my eyes. *What to wear? What about my hair? What will Cliff think of me now?*

I walked to my closet and surveyed clothes I hadn't worn for a while. The first dress I tried on, hung on me like a sack of potatoes. *Old potatoes.* I had to wear a dress because Cliff loved my legs and I needed all the ammo I could muster.

I looked in the mirror and realized I would also need "the works."

So, I called the beauty salon, and booked an appointment for a color, cut and style.

If I tried my best, maybe I could at least look somewhat like the gal Cliff had fallen in love with.

After my appointment at the salon, and the manicurist, I did look better, not great.

I wanted to buy a new dress badly, but I didn't have much money, considering I'd quit my job.

I wondered if guys noticed if a dress fit well or not.

Hopefully, Cliff will just be staring at my freshly cut and colored hair, and not the dress!

Chapter Twenty
CLIFFORD

November 1984

I chose the same cozy Italian restaurant we had frequented so often. It was never very crowded. I didn't need any distractions. I had to keep my mind on the task. I couldn't add the poison to Maddie's drink at the restaurant. I had to invite her back to my place. *It should be easy enough to convince her to have an after-dinner drink.* But the more I thought about it, that I was taking the next step in the plan, the more my hands grew clammy and my stomach cramped.

You're considering MURDER, Cliff. Hope you realize how terrible this plan of action is!! My thoughts shouted at me.

I turned every step of the plan over in my mind. *Should we have sex?* I didn't know if it would make me feel worse, and I didn't know if I could feel worse. I doubted it. I hated her, but I suspected I detested myself more.

The restaurant hostess seated me at a table in the back corner. I didn't want anyone to see us together. I noticed a small candle burning in the center of the table. Good, hopefully, Maddie wouldn't be able to read the anxiety on my face, in the semi-darkness. I had to appear calm and relaxed. Almost happy, if possible.

Maybe everything I was hatching wasn't such a good idea. What if Ernie came strolling in? What if Annie or anyone else we knew showed up? Annie couldn't resist coming over to our table to "chat."

I wore the same sports jacket I had worn the night we met. I wondered if Madeline would remember and if I would start perspiring again. *Maybe the jacket was a mistake?*

So many times, I replayed in my mind how the evening would go, and one thing was certain. I wanted her to feel something. Maybe for her just to understand how she had hurt me so terribly, how she had hurt me when I had trusted her with every fiber of my heart.

Every time I recalled how Maddie excited me, I felt like an absolute fool all over again to have fallen for such a lie. *Would anyone else have been taken in as easily as me?* And I still thought of Ernie. How I had felt we were friends and that all had been forgiven so long ago, never knowing that Ernie had just gotten madder and madder. I would never have suspected Ernie was plotting so hard, that he would be okay destroying me. I had fallen into his snare as easily as a mouse throws itself on a block of cheese in a spring-loaded trap.

Then Madeline finally appeared.

So far, so good.

She looked terrible for the first time in her life. She had lost a lot of weight since I had last seen her and was tired. Almost ill. *What if my plans go haywire again? What if she has a terminal illness?* Instead of feeling pity; I raged silently. *I will be doing all of this for nothing.*

Madeline's dress was periwinkle blue and was not the same one I had first seen her in. Her dress looked too large for her. It was short, but despite her thin frame, I still couldn't pull my eyes away from her unforgettable legs.

When she walked toward me, I felt nothing. Her approach did not have the same effect on me as it had that first night. Maybe I was too caught up in what I was about to do. My stomach churned, and I prayed my eye wouldn't twitch, or worse, that I wouldn't get one of my headaches.

Maddie smiled, and I rose from the table. She gave me a slight hug, and I stood there, wooden inside and out. My emotions swirled everywhere in my body. As I took in her frail beauty, I couldn't believe what I was planning. *I am going to kill her.* Not that she didn't have it coming. But to die? It was quite extreme, for sure!

How could I hate her and love her at the same time?

Pretty crazy. I had cracked. And I knew it.

We ordered drinks. A Cosmo for Maddie and an Old Style for me. Then we tried to make small, small talk, but it was awkward.

The conversation did not come easily. We fidgeted in our chairs and felt no magical ambiance.

We ordered dinner and the night went on with the dawning realization that time was moving along. Suddenly, dinner was over, and I was growing more and more nervous by the minute. It was hard to hold my bottle of beer. My palms were too slick.

After dinner, I paid the check and followed Maddie outside. Then I asked her if she wanted to come home with me and I held my breath as I waited for her answer. *What if she refused?*

Maddie thanked me and said that she thought it would be lovely.

Lovely, huh?

She had no idea of the hate brewing inside me.

When we got back to my place, we sat in opposite chairs. I suggested that Maddie make herself comfortable, while I prepared drinks. Once in the kitchen, I mixed a Cosmo for Maddie and another Old Style for myself. I had broken the Abrin beads earlier, and I very carefully handled the powder so as not to kill myself through contact with it, then I poured it into Maddie's drink.

We sat and sipped. I played some music, and one of Maddie's favorite songs came on. "Truly," was the song I had heard the night I met Maddie.

Instead of going all gooey inside like the moment I had laid eyes on her, I couldn't help but laugh to myself about how ridiculous the lyrics sounded now, considering all the deception. My mind worked overtime. I decided against sex because I didn't think I could handle the emotional part.

Maddie kept sipping her drink. I couldn't wait for her to finish it! But I worried about what would happen when she did.

When she got to the last drop, I didn't know if I was relieved or even more anxious.

As the minutes went on, I knew the poison would take hold. I made a weak excuse that I had to get up early the next morning and then asked her, "Would it be alright if I called a cab for you?"

The sooner I could push her out the door, the better, because I didn't want to be with her when the poison kicked in and the clock was ticking!

She agreed, but when I walked her to the door, she grabbed my hand and then turned me around to face her. She pulled me close and gave me a long, lingering kiss. I couldn't believe that I didn't feel a damn thing. None of the old feelings. I guessed I was too full of hate, revenge, and misery by then.

A few tears rolled down Maddie's face as she told me she still loved me.

"Maybe we can start fresh? I know it's you I truly [there's that word again] love," Maddie sighed.

"How about we discuss this another time?" I suggested. *Man, she's dragging this out. Why won't she leave?*

Maddie nodded her head in agreement, and softly said, "Alright."

Then, I closed the door, and she was gone! I leaned my damp forehead against the wall, knowing I had just committed the most despicable act. *Why was I not consumed with guilt? What was the matter with me?* I was submerged in total self-loathing. *Where was Mr. Nice Guy? Had he disappeared forever?*

Chapter Twenty-One
ERNIE

November 1984

I had taken the night off work and waited for Maddie at the apartment. We hadn't seen each other a lot since the blow up although we still lived together for the time being. I didn't want to get drunk again. I knew the minute I would see her, I would start a huge argument.

Maddie finally made it to the apartment. The first thing I accused her of was sleeping around.

"Where the hell have you been? No call, no thoughts of maybe it would be nice to let Ernie know where I am, and what time I will be home? No, not a thought for ol' Ern."

What spewed out of my mouth was unreal. I told her I hated her, had never loved her and that I would be glad to be rid of her.

The more I looked at her cheating face, the more enraged I became. I had been foolish to think that what we had going for us, could withstand anything. Even my crazy scheme with Cliff. I certainly didn't think she would betray me and fall for Cliff!

"Are you happy now? Do you really think Cliff loves you enough to forgive you? Well, you had better think that one over again. It ain't gonna happen, baby. Cliff will never forgive you, never. He probably hates your cheating face as much as I do. Get ready for some big fireworks, because they are coming your way!" I seethed into her white face.

"It's a good turn of events, this whole crapfest." I went on.

Yeah, her pretty white face, I wanted to sock her right in the middle of it.

I grabbed her arm, resisting the urge to twist it until she screamed and hung on as tight as I could.

"Ernie, let go! You're hurting me! You're drunk!"

"No, baby, I will not let go of you! I am staying here with you in this apartment. We are going to have a nice long talk, or at the very least, have this problem solved once and for all."

It felt good saying the words, so I kept going. "You are probably the worst bitch I've ever met in my entire life."

Chapter Twenty-Two
MADELINE

November 1984

So now, I am the "worst bitch" Ernie ever met in his life!?

I doubt that. He's out of control, even more than his usual drunkenness.

My mind raced. The only good effect that had come out of the unreal scheme was meeting and falling in love with Cliff. Now, he had given me another chance. I would prove to him with my whole heart that I would be faithful. If he let me, I would love him forever! Now, if I could contend with the crazy version of Ernie hanging around the apartment!

Ernie lounged on the couch with the weirdest expression on his face. Then he got up and walked into the kitchen. He opened the fridge and then a beer. I don't think it was his first.

"Why don't you slip into something more comfortable? You know ... for ol' time's sake?"

"Ernie, I told you, you're drunk. I want you to leave," I said, dread rising, a wobble in my voice. I took a step backward from him.

"You're acting all freakish, and you are scaring me." I didn't care if he knew I was afraid. I just wanted him out.

Then the most heated argument started. Ernie accusing me of sleeping around, and more.

Suddenly, Ernie grabbed my arm, and held on! He wouldn't let go.

I finally pulled away, but he kept on with the argument, saying every vile thing about me he could.

"Did you really think I could ever love you again after everything you've done? I hate you. I loathe you. I detest you," Ernie said, with the darkest eyes I have ever seen. "Too bad, baby. It's all over for you. In more ways than one."

I ran for our bedroom. At least, I could lock myself inside until Ernie gave up and left. As I raced away from him, I heard a terrible BOOM. A sudden stinging pain in my neck knocked me to my knees.

Chapter Twenty-Three
CLIFFORD

November 1984

What kind of monster have I become? I wondered as I muddled through my usual morning routine the night after I had poisoned Maddie.

I had driven to the morgue and vaguely recalled arriving. It was early, and I wanted to get the day over with, so I could go home and wallow in my misery and suffocating remorse.

Annie was there like usual. Only this morning wasn't as it always had been, and never would be again.

Ready to jump out of my skin and into my lab coat, I prayed that if Madeline's body were waiting, on a tray, that Annie would *oh please, oh please NOT pull the tray with Maddie on it!* But of course, as had happened with everything I had screwed up in my life, Maddie's tray was pulled. *I would be the one to work on Maddie!!!*

As I walked in, Annie cracked her gum. She did not, however, have her customary grin on her face.

I proceeded to make the first cut on Madeline's porcelain chest, and Annie said, "Why don't you roll this beauty over? She's got a bullet lodged in her silky white neck. Guess it killed her instantly."

Annie adjusted one of her gloves giving me time to urge the color to my cheeks. I knew without looking; my complexion was paste. I couldn't catch my breath and had to grip the cold metal table to anchor me to reality.

My head swam as Annie continued, "It was all over the morning papers. Our pal, Ernie shot her. Can you believe it? How could a sweet guy like Ern do something as horrible as this?"

ACKNOWLEDGMENTS

First and foremost, I want to thank my amazing, awesome daughters, Cathy and Wendy. Their love and encouragement during this entire journey has been unwavering. They have been my parachute, telling me I can soar and always keeping me grounded. *I love you more than you know!*

Also, a huge thanks to my four wonderful grandchildren — Jenny, Christine, Brian and Janet — for encouraging Nana to keep going. *Love you!* And ... my two adorable great-grandchildren — Madison and Jackson — for making me realize that yes, life does go on. *Such a joy!* And to all my many friends — and one very SPECIAL friend — your enthusiasm for me is so appreciated. *I love all of you!*

Without my fantastic editor, Hilary Jastram, and my equally fantastic publisher, Kate Colbert, this manuscript would still be sitting in a drawer. You stayed with me and showed me "I could do it!" *Thank you for your patience and wisdom.*

ABOUT THE AUTHOR

Shirley Guendling, a lifelong children's book author, is excited to have written her first full-length novel at the young age of 88 years. Shirley grew up in Chicago, Illinois, during the Great Depression and later moved to the suburbs where she met her late husband Donald and they had  two beautiful daughters. After her two children and four grandchildren got older, Shirley was not ready to slow down and took on a job at her local library, where she has now been working for more than 20 years surrounded by what she loves most ... books.

Her love for literature and expansive imagination led her to envision Cliff and Maddie, and she knew theirs was a story she had to write. *I Believed You*, a whirlwind romance thriller, pulls inspiration from Shirley's life experiences, although it is mostly fiction. Shirley had to teach herself how to use a computer and word processing software in her 80s to pursue her dreams of writing her own books, but she was determined to do it.

Shirley's social calendar is often booked weeks in advance, as she loves spending time with cherished friends and most importantly, her family. She is an avid reader, reading 1-2 novels a week and loves the cultural arts. Her passion for writing keeps her busy, and she is always dreaming up new characters and plots. She belongs to several book writing and critique clubs and is hard at work on her second novel.

Connect with Shirley at sguendling4429@sbcglobal.net.